To. Scott

From Papa & Nan

xmas 1986

Favourite
Bedtime
Stories

Favourite Bedtime Stories

Translated by Susie Saunders

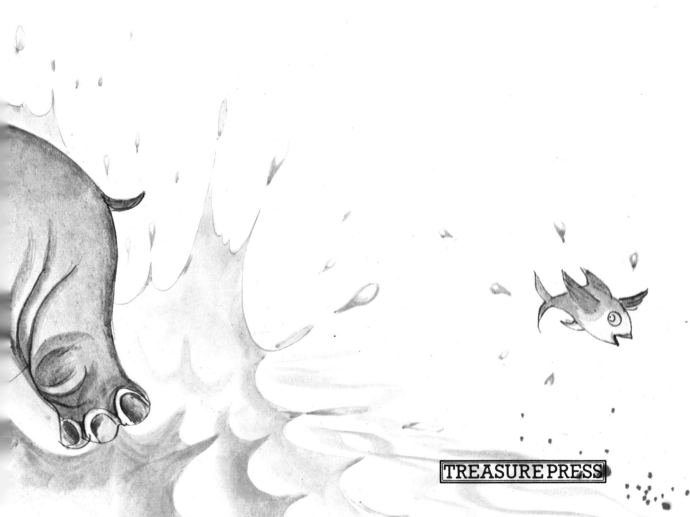

TREASURE PRESS

Contents

First published in Great Britain by Octopus Books Ltd
This edition published in 1983 by Treasure Press
59 Grosvenor Street
London W1
Reprinted 1986

© 1977 Litor Publishers Ltd, Brighton
This edition © 1978 Octopus Books Ltd
ISBN 0 907812 34 1
Printed in Czechoslovakia
50350/4

The Magic Animals of the Merry-go-round

The blue horse on the merry-go-round was carrying his last passenger of the day. He looked very tired.

Peter was on his back and spurring him on. 'Come on, blue horse,' he cried, as if he knew the horse was tired, 'only one more lap to go and then we can all sleep.'

With a grunt and a groan the merry-go-round finally stopped and the blue horse sighed deeply.

'Hooray! We've won,' giggled Peter, 'thanks for going so fast, blue horse.'

'I'm tired of going round and round in the same old circle. I long to gallop over the fields and meadows like other horses. Perhaps you could help, sir?'

Peter blushed. He had never been called 'sir' before. 'Please call me Peter, blue horse . . . and I'll help you in any way I can. What do you want me to do?'

'It's very easy. Come back here tonight and untie the ropes to the canvas that covers the merry-go-round.'

and I'll give you the ride of your life.'

So Peter went back when the moon was high in the sky. He undid the canvas ropes and soon the blue horse and his best friends were free.

The blue horse sniffed the fragrant hay and the sweet-scented night air, and shook his golden mane impatiently. 'Jump up Peter, and let's get going!'

They galloped along the road which passed the windmill. They were a strange sight in the moonlight; a happy, multicoloured procession of animals. There was Peter and the blue horse; the rosy pink pig with the corkscrew tail and laughing face; a grey donkey with long silvery ears . . . and a spotted cow who wanted to eat the green grass.

By and by, the friends from the merry-go-round gathered in a clearing at the edge of the wood where they spotted a quaint cottage.

'What then, blue horse?'

'Wait and see,' replied the blue horse, mysteriously.

'If you go somewhere nice, can I come too?'

'Yes, you can climb on my back

7

'Is this where the witch lives?' asked the blue horse.

Peter laughed. 'Somebody much nicer than a witch lives here. This is the home of Rosemary the herb-mother.'

Just then the door of the cottage opened and Rosemary called out to the surprised party, 'Hello, my friends. Please come in.'

It was a tight squeeze in the small low-ceilinged cottage, but one by one Peter and the animals went in and made themselves right at home.

'Would you like some buckwheat pancakes?' Rosemary asked.

Peter's eyes shone and he clapped his hands with glee. 'We'll make them, herb-mother,' he said at once.

'Indeed we'll make them,' echoed the blue horse. 'Just sit down in your rocking chair. You're in for a treat.'

The pink pig blew on the sleeping embers.

8

Peter broke the eggs into a bowl.

The spotted cow poured in the flour.

The blue horse mixed in the milk.

All the animals busied themselves doing something to help make the pancakes.

At last the mixture was ready.

All the animals watched the blue horse pour some of the mixture into the frying pan. 'Everyone can have a turn,' the blue horse said. 'Just watch carefully as I toss the pancake.' The horse flicked his hooves and the pancake sailed towards the ceiling and then down again, right into the middle of the pan.

'Hooray!' the herb-mother said and clapped her hands. 'Blue horse, fetch the pots of jam from the sideboard.'

While the blue horse fetched the jam, the others took turns in making the pancakes.

Peter opened the jam pots and dipped his finger into each one. 'Ooh! Raspberries, blackberries, blackcurrants and rhubarb!'

'Grey donkey,' said Rosemary, 'please uncork the bottles of cider.'

Pop! Pop! The cider bubbled out in a white froth on to the table.

The herb-mother busied herself finding glasses for everyone.

After their feast, the pink pig went for a little snooze in the straw with the spotted cow. From time to time, the grey donkey and the blue horse ran off into the deep silence of the night to race right around the clover field. Peter stayed with the herb-mother and did the washing-up. He also licked out the jam pots.

All too soon the friends saw the first pink glow at the edge of the sky.

'Come,' said the blue horse sadly, 'it's time to go back to the merry-go-round.'

Soon, Peter was saying good-night to his new friends. 'I'll come back often,' he promised.

I wonder where the animals of the merry-go-round have gone tonight?

9

The Blue Blackbird

'Off I fly, one two three, off to raid the cherry tree,' whistled Blackie cheerfully on a beautiful clear morning.

The orchard was not far away and the cherry trees were groaning under the weight of their round red fruit. Some sparrows and several blackbirds were already feasting on them.

'Oh!' said Blackie. 'They're not going to leave any for me. I'll have to hurry!'

Blackie's greediness sped him along so fast that, with wings flapping wildly, he flew straight into the trunk of the cherry tree, and fell with a heavy thud into a pot of blue emulsion.

'It feels horrible and it's so sticky!' cried Blackie as he struggled to get out of the pot. The sun was hot and soon the paint had dried all over him.

In despair Blackie started crying and calling his friends to help him.

'We're coming,' his brother blackbirds whistled happily.

The little sparrows heard the blackbirds and they, too, flew to Blackie, their tummies crammed full of cherries.

When they saw Blackie looking so strange, the other blackbirds and the sparrows couldn't help laughing.

'Aren't you funny!' they whistled.
And the sparrows chirped in
chorus: 'Cheep, cheep, cheep, cheep,
you do look odd!'

Blackie sobbed even harder and
wondered what on earth he must look
like. But the paint just wouldn't
shift even though they all tried to
peck it off.

'Oh well,' he sighed, as he dried
his tears, 'I'll just have to put up
with it.'

Blackie flew to a nearby pond and
studied his reflection. 'Um,' he said,
with a satisfied whistle, 'I think I
look rather good.' The other blackbirds weren't so sure, but there was
one bird who thought him very handsome and couldn't help saying so.
She was Snowy, the most beautiful
white dove Blackie had ever seen.

It was a pity about the rain coming.
It poured down so fiercely that
Blackie was soon washed black again.
The beautiful dove took one look at
him and flew away.

'Oh well,' sighed Blackie, 'I sup-
pose I'd better find my friends. At
least they like me black.'

The Mischievous Lamb

How pretty the frisky little white lamb with the black face and dainty feet looked!

He followed the other sheep of the marshes, grazing the salty grass that the sea covered on high tide days.

That evening, the sea would hide the marsh and turn it into a big silver lake. The white seagulls flew overhead, calling to the slower sheep, 'Come along you dawdlers, get off the marsh.'

Oliver, the shepherd, shooed his sheep towards the sandhills. 'Ten, twelve, fourteen, sixteen, eighteen, nineteen!' the young boy counted. 'There's one missing! Where's the black-faced lamb?'

'Oh!' cried Helen, Oliver's sister. 'We must find him quickly.'

The children rushed on to a sand-hill overlooking the marsh.

'I can't see anything,' said Helen.

'Perhaps he's behind the reeds,' replied Oliver, 'I'll go and look.'

'And I'll go round the sheep huts in case our little wanderer has gone with the wrong flock.'

The sea came up and covered most of the grass leaving only one or two little green islands.

But where was the black-faced lamb? There didn't seem to be any place for him to hide himself away. But Oliver could not see him.

The black-faced lamb was pran-

cing in a carrot field. What a lovely outing and what a marvellous time the little wanderer was having!

The black-faced lamb tasted a drop of the water that was tickling his feet. Ugh! Too salty!

Soon the water covered his knees. 'Baaa . . . baaa . . . baaa . . . baaa,' cried the lonely lamb.

'There he is!' cried Oliver.

'He'll drown if we don't hurry,' said Helen, 'poor little lamb.'

'Come on,' cried Oliver, 'we must get to the other side of the marsh. Bring the dog.'

What a mad dash! Racing over the bridge, the road, the rushes.

They finally made it, but no amount of calling would get the lamb into the water so they sent the dog to coax the lamb back.

The dog dived into the water and swam bravely to the island that was already under water.

'Baaa . . . baaa,' bleated the black-faced lamb in desperation. But then the dog barked behind him and the lamb jumped into the water.

'He's swimming at last!'

'Come on, little one, come on.'

They weren't sure if he would be strong enough to reach them, but there was nothing they could do.

Finally the lamb pulled himself out of the water and dropped at their feet with exhaustion. Helen gently picked up the soaking wet lamb and hugged him to her.

The black-faced lamb would come when he was called the next time.

Porky and Dino Have Fun

'Let's play at being silly today,' suggested Dino, the little donkey, to his friend Porky, the pig.

'I know! We can scare the hens!'

No sooner said than done. What a lot of bewildered squawking!

The donkey and the pig beamed with glee. They beamed even more when some eggs smashed on the floor.

'What a lovely omelette,' said Dino.

Attracted by the smell of the broken eggs, Ferdy the Fox came creeping up without a sound. What a feast!

'Thank you,' he said to Porky and Dino. 'Oh, what it is to have friends like you.'

14

But Porky and Dino did not hear a word. They were running right into the middle of a flock of sheep.

'Baaa! Baaa!' bleated the lambs.

'Woof! Woof!' barked Griff, the dog.

But Griff's protests were in vain. Dino and Porky then turned their attention to the farmhouse kitchen and had great delight in spilling the contents of the fridge all over the floor.

As a finishing touch, Dino put a copper cauldron on his head like a hat, and ran out to the farmyard.

'You are such a laugh!' hooted Porky.

But the cauldron fell off on to the foot of the big, strong, bull.

'Ow!' the bull roared in fury.

The two naughty animals looked meekly at the enraged bull. Perhaps they hadn't been so funny after all.

'I've been watching you two all day,' the bull said to the trembling pair. 'And now you can go into the kitchen and clear up all the mess!'

The Adventures of Maude the Mole

Maude the mole was all a-flutter. 'Sniff, sniff,' she said to herself, twitching her nose, 'I can smell spring. Let's have a look!'

Maude put on her spectacles, because her eyesight wasn't very good in the daylight, and stuck the tip of her snout outside. It was a bright and beautiful day. Spring had really arrived.

A careless little ray of sunshine reflected on Maude's spectacles. 'Hey,' she protested, 'you don't have to blind me altogether.'

But finally Maude plucked up enough courage to go out of her hole. Two steps, three steps . . . her head was spinning, but she managed to see the blue sky and the birds flying close to her.

But crash! Maude had fallen over on the soft grass next to a clump of primroses, all wet from the night.

'Hello Maude,' said the flowers.

By the time she had staggered to her feet again, Maude discovered she was near the stream where the ducks were sailing happily along.

'Hello, ducks,' said the mole, 'it's spring you know.'

'We do know,' quacked the ducks, 'our eggs are already laid!'

'Cuckoo,' said the cuckoo, ready for a game of hide-and-seek.

Maude refrained from answering because there were lots of things she wanted to see and to do.

For a start she decided to follow the little stream, on top of a box which would act as her boat.

Maude hadn't sailed far when she

got stuck in the reeds. With fear in her heart, Maude called for help with all her might.

A wild goose kindly gave Maude a ride to the bank on his back, advising, 'Walk the rest of the way, it will be much safer.'

'I will, I promise,' said Maude, still shaking with fright.

Maude realised then that she was very hungry and started to look for food. She didn't have to look far and found plenty to choose from.

Suddenly Maude felt sad as she watched the birds flying all around her. 'I would like to fly like the birds and what's more, I'm going to try.' And so Maude climbed on to a hillock and flapped her legs. 'One, two, three, here we go, let's use all our brain and muscles!' she called,

as she flew through the air. Then with a crash and a bang Maude had landed . . . on the ground. Then she rolled and she rolled, right into the duck pond.

Once again Maude cried for help. She hated that strange watery world. Soon a hedgehog pushed out a reed that Maude hung on to with all her might. When she reached dry land Maude started to cry, then she thanked the hedgehog.

A friendly squirrel plaited her a crown of daisies and the frogs started to clap.

Soon Maude was smiling again. 'Never again will I try to be a sailor, or a bird, or anything else,' she told her friends. 'I think from now on I will be happy being a mole with not very good eyesight.'

17

The Day of the Fair

The hot summer sun had ripened the hay, and the farmer was anxious to gather it into his barn. 'Quick, to work,' said the farmer. 'Giddy up, Hilda, get a move on!'

From dawn till dusk, Hilda the mare pulled the long cart full of fragrant hay for her master.

Trot, the donkey, carried the heavy milk churns to the dairy. 'You're so lucky, you pink pig,' he said, 'to be splashing around in the cool mud. And you, ducks, to be swimming in the cold water of the pond.' Trot would have given anything to be relieved of his duties.

Then the day of the fair came and the farm animals decided to take a well-earned rest. They got all dressed up and went happily off without so much as saying a word to the farmer. But Hilda and Trot had worked hard all summer and deserved a reward.

What high spirits the two animals were in as they trotted along the white road lined with daisies and poppies.

They forgot all about the work to be done, and went towards the fair without a care in the world.

'Where are you going?' asked the curious cows.

'To the fair. Come with us!'

'Where are you going?' asked the other donkeys and horses.

'To the fair. Come with us!'

'Where are you going?' asked the goats and their prancing kids.

'To the fair. Come with us!'

The ewes and their curly lambs followed them too, munching at the banks of clover and sweet grass.

At each step of the way they collected more and more animals, all eager to join the fun of the fair.

At last they reached the fair with its merry-go-round.

The cows rushed to the swings and the calves made for the merry-go-round.

A little tan and white calf pulled a tassel from the merry-go-round. He looked around worriedly, but as everybody laughed he started laughing too and clapped his hands.

The horses and the donkeys jumped into the dodgem cars. They liked driving into each other. Bang! Crash! What fun!

They turned; they spinned; they thumped; they collided. They got a bit scared and shouted. Then they laughed and went off again. One more go and then another . . .

Some felt they had never had so much fun in their lives!

The sheep and the crazy goats were too timid to do anything but watch to start with, then finally reassured, they jumped on to a merry-go-round. They each chose a plane, a car, a bus or a boat.

'Push the lever!' shouted a sheep.

Whee! The plane went up. 'Good-bye! Good-bye!'

'Do you think the plane will come down again?' asked the ewe.

'Why don't we go right up to the sky!' suggested the sheep, laughing.

'Oh no! My lambs, my baby lambs are still down there!' cried the ewe.

'There now: I'll push this and we're going down. Now back up again!'

The ewe soon lost her nervousness in the excitement of the ride in the sky.

The horses and the donkeys had moved from the dodgem cars to the rifle range.

'Hilda has won!' came the cry. 'Well done! A bottle of lemonade!'

The white goat had also won a prize. It was a big pink doll with a beautifully worked lace dress.

'Look over there!' called the donkey. 'A singing contest!'

'Go on, Trot. You've got a nice voice. We dare you to get up on the stage!'

All the contestants were lining up and clearing their throats in readiness. All Trot's friends felt sure he could win.

Trot hesitated. He was afraid they would all make fun of him. But his friends gave him one big push and there he was in front of the audience. Trot sang one of his prettiest songs. It was about the summer and fragrant hay, and about the joy of being loved.

What applause the audience gave to Trot! He blushed to the tips of his ears. When they voted him the winner, his friends cheered in delight.

Later on, there was dancing on the grass. There was much throwing of balloons and pretty coloured streamers. It was very late when everyone started to go home.

I wonder if they were too tired to work the next day?

The Goat and the Sun

Glenda, the goat, was in her paddock showing her two pointed horns to the newly-risen sun.

The sun was as round as an enormous red ball so that Glenda wanted to play with it.

'If only I could catch it,' she said to herself. 'That would be fun. It's on top of the hill. I'll go and fetch it!'

Glenda jumped easily over the fence and climbed the long winding path. Nibbling a little thyme here, a leaf from a bush there, she stopped just long enough to catch her breath before skipping and leaping on again.

Glenda arrived on the top of the hill, but where was the sun? Why!

It was way down in the valley.

'It's not possible, it's not believable,' Glenda complained. 'When I was in the valley, it was on top of the hill! And now it's in the valley.'

Glenda didn't feel like playing any more. In fact, she was quite woebegone. 'Why did the sun run away? I only wanted it for my ball!'

Despairingly, Glenda hung her head and sobbed.

Molly the mole tried to reason

21

with her: 'You can't just catch the sun,' she explained.

Glenda sobbed even harder.

The kind mole asked the advice of the frogs, but they couldn't help, so they asked the friendly birds. 'Please ask the sun to be Glenda's ball.'

The birds flew up close to the sun and begged it to help Glenda the goat.

The sun laughed and turned one of its rays into a bright ball that the north wind cooled at once.

What joy for Glenda! Now she had her very own sun ball! What fun she had! She pranced and ran, the shining ball balancing on the tip of her horns.

There she goes . . . one, two, three, up in the air . . . Glenda tossed the ball up high and then caught it cleverly with her horns. But once she didn't catch it, and the ball went rolling away and, with a last bounce, it landed in the blue water of the lake.

The lake shone like a mirror and one by one, the animals came to look at their reflections in the water. The swan was the most handsome.

Glenda forgot all about the red ball floating in the water. It was time to play with her friends.

Scamp Goes Shopping

'Listen, Scamp,' said Sandra. 'We're going to give Mummy a lovely surprise today.'

'Good idea,' agreed Scamp. 'What can I do to help?'

'You can go to the market and buy eight fat sausages.'

Scamp proudly picked up the basket with his teeth and went off to market. There he asked the butcher, 'Can I have eight fat sausages please?'

Sandra waited anxiously at home. It was nearly lunchtime but where was Scamp? Scamp was having problems. As he left the market, one, two, three dogs jumped on him.

'Catch him! We'll have those sausages!' yelled the leader.

Scamp ran as fast as his legs would carry him.

He raced into the park but the dogs behind him barked, 'Woof! Woof! Pant! Woof!' They were hot on his heels.

Scamp dashed on to the road. Bang! He dropped the basket and the sausages fell to the ground. Scamp grabbed them and stuffed them back in the basket.

'Woof! Woof! Gasp! Gasp! Woof!' went the dogs behind him.

Scamp jumped on to a lorry which was just drawing away from the kerb. 'Fooled you, didn't I?' he

23

yelled to the dogs behind him. Then he discovered that the lorry was going in the wrong direction and he had to jump off.

Scamp ran along the railway line, the dogs barking at his heels.

Then came a terrible noise . . . chuff . . . chuff . . . Vroom!

A train was coming. Scamp tried to escape but he could turn neither left nor right.

Scamp lay down flat on the sleepers and made himself as small as possible, his head between his paws.

There was an awful din above him, a terrible never-ending racket.

A long goods train thundered above him, with all its coaches loaded with lovely new cars. Scamp didn't see them though. He had even nearly forgotten about the sausages.

At last the train had passed!

Scamp lifted his head. The train had disappeared and so had the dogs. Whoosh, he whizzed by the market like an arrow and all the way home.

'There you are, Scamp, whatever happened to you?'

'It's a long story, Sandra, but I'll tell you later,' Scamp answered mysteriously.

'Quick, we must hurry. Mummy will be home soon.'

'I hope the sausages will be good!' said Scamp, still panting.

'But look, they're so dirty,' cried Sandra. 'That's nothing,' Scamp said; 'once I've grilled them, they'll be all brown and you won't see the dirt.'

Nevertheless, Sandra washed them all the same.

When Mummy got home everything was ready. Even the dish of mashed potato with the sausages on top.

'This is delicious, Sandra. You are a marvellous cook,' she said with approval.

'Scamp helped me a lot.'

The little dog jumped into the arms of his friend, who gave him a kiss. He did not let on that they nearly didn't have any sausages.

Lucy's Special Christmas

Today was a very special day. It was Christmas, and Lucy was very busy preparing a special celebration dinner and decorating the tree with candles, streamers and tinsel. The curtains were drawn and from the outside the room looked warm, pretty and inviting.

Suddenly she noticed two bright eyes watching her through the window. It was Smoky, a poor dog whose master had disappeared and who had been roaming about sadly ever since, in search of food and affection.

Lucy took pity on him and called, 'Come in, Smoky! Please spend Christmas with us!'

Smoky was taken aback, and asked shyly, 'Can I bring my friends along, the squirrel, the owl, and the field-mouse?'

'All your friends are welcome here,' Lucy replied at once.

What a warm and friendly party there was that Christmas Day.

And what happy times there were after that, for Smoky and his friends never left that pretty thatched cottage in the woods. And every Christmas after that was happy.

Little Finch and the Red Rose

Little Finch, perched on an oak branch, watched the sun rise. But, to his great dismay, he could not sing a note.

'What's the matter?' asked Perky the sparrow.

'I've got a cold,' said Little Finch. 'And a sore throat,' he croaked.

In despair, he went to see his friend Red Rose, the Queen of the Garden.

'Good morning, Red Rose,' he whispered.

But instead of his usual warm welcome he received a sad greeting from Red Rose.

'Ah . . . Ah . . . tchoo!' said Red Rose. 'Ah . . . Ah . . . tchoo!'

'Have you by any chance got a cold too?' asked Little Finch.

'Ah . . . tchoo!' Can't you see I have!' grumbled the flower, tired after a sleepness night.

The other finches and garden flowers were sad. They would have to do something, for they knew that if Red Rose and Little Finch were not cured soon, all the flowers and creatures of the garden would fall ill too.

So the finches hurried to see the bees.

'Red Rose and Little Finch have got colds. Can you help them?'

'Bzzz, bzzz,' droned the bees. They did not hear for they were too busy making honey.

'I'll go to see the sun,' twittered the lark brightly.

She was a bird who always liked to be helpful, and she was sad to see her friends feeling so ill.

She flew as high as she could and plucked a nice warm beam as she passed.

The beam warmed the Little Finch's feathers and dried the dew from Red Rose's heart. It shone once more and spread joy all around.

'I'm cured!' exclaimed Red Rose happily.

'Me too,' sang Little Finch.

His notes wafted joyously into the clear sky. He laughed whole-heartedly and danced for joy with the butterflies, the flowers and all the birds. The whole of their little world was happy again.

Little Finch felt he must do something to show all the birds how grateful he was. So Little Finch led his friends the birds to the balcony of a house where there were lots of seeds.

It was a real feast!

When night fell, the birds returned to their nests and the warm little beam hurried back to the sun.

All the birds and flowers felt much better going to bed than they had that morning.

Little Finch said good-bye to Red Rose.

Then he went to say a special thank you to the little lark who had helped so willingly.

The Bear and the Goose

In a big pine forest, there lived in perfect harmony Kola the little bear, and Gertie the grey goose.

They had known each other since they were born and each day brought a new adventure for them.

Now Kola was a greedy bear. He was always looking for strawberries, raspberries and blackberries.

Getting honey, which he adored, was quite a business, and the bees defended themselves as best they could.

'Bzzz, bzzz . . .' they all sang as they stung Kola's nose.

They were awful! Kola was not at

all happy when that happened.

One morning Kola discovered a lovely honeycomb.

The little bear was very hungry. The bees were nowhere to be seen. Now was the time for action!

'I'll warn you as soon as they come back,' promised Gertie.

She was a kind goose and was always ready to help her friend. So now she looked right, left, ahead, and behind . . . but she could see no bees.

Kola was quietly having a feast. He gobbled away without a care in the world. He was covered in honey.

'Goodness!' exclaimed Gertie, amazed. 'You'll have to wash.'

She dragged her friend, full up and sticky as he was, to the big river where the beautiful salmon were swimming.

Kola, as greedy as ever, gobbled one up as it swam past.

'Wash yourself,' ordered Gertie. 'You're all sticky.'

The goose decided to bath too and swam around in the water.

'Who can swim the fastest?' asked Gertie slyly.

'Me!' replied Kola, very sure of himself and falling for the trick.

'We'll see,' said Gertie.

Gertie swam very fast and won.

Shamefaced, Kola climbed out of the water and dried himself.

Meanwhile, the bees had arrived back at their tree and were very cross. 'Look!' exclaimed the Queen Bee, 'our honey has disappeared. Kola's taken it.

'Let's teach him a lesson once and for all.'

Gertie spotted the bees first and she nudged Kola frantically. Before she could say anything, the bear threw himself into the water again.

'Phew, saved!' thought Kola.

Later on, the two friends came to a pleasant spot and decided to stay a while.

They watched as some frogs leaped over a high fence.

'I'm going to do that,' said Kola.

The frogs croaked with laughter. 'You're a big fat lump, croak, croak. You couldn't jump over a log!'

Kola and Gertie left the unfriendly frogs far behind and went to see some beavers who had built a raft.

'Let us test it!' implored Gertie and Kola.

What fun! The raft floated well and moved fast. But suddenly it was caught in the current.

Gertie jumped off in time, but Kola fell into the water and was washed over a waterfall. But he escaped with only a very small bruise.

Before the two friends had decided what to do next, Kola spotted the bees.

What a chase followed! The bees were so cross that they stung anything that got in their way, including a squirrel and a badger.

But soon the friends had reached the safety of the bear's cave.

Gertie prepared a wood fire on which they grilled a salmon.

'What a hectic day! Perhaps tomorrow will be better,' said Gertie.

'I hope so,' said Kola, gobbling up the salmon. 'Anyway, I think I'd better not steal any more honey for a while.'

Johnny Rabbit's Star

Johnny Rabbit, all round and brown, was madly in love with a beautiful star. When night fell, his eyes turned up to heaven, and he gazed at his sweetheart.

From high up in the sky, the star blew him kisses in return.

When Johnny Rabbit washed in the river, he could see her reflection in the water.

She followed him everywhere, as if she were lonely without him.

How they would have loved to meet!

But alas! The sky was so high and the earth so far away. How could the two friends possibly be united? It seemed impossible.

When he could stand it no longer, Johnny Rabbit went to see the Chief of the Brown Rabbit tribe. Perhaps the Chief Rabbit could give him some advice on how to solve his terrible dilemma.

The Chief was at a loss. So he called the Chief of the Squirrels and told him about Johnny Rabbit's plight. What could be done to unite a rabbit and a star?

Nobody seemed to have any idea.

Nobody had ever heard of such a thing before.

But wait! Surely the big cedar tree in the clearing reached up to the sky? They all laughed, happy to have found an answer to Johnny Rabbit's problem.

Wasting no time, they tied Johnny securely to the end of a rope, and the Brown Rabbit colony was ordered to pull on the rope, whilst the Squirrel tribe pushed him up to the top of the tree.

Alas! The top of the tree, high as it was, was still a long way from the stars. What a disappointment for Johnny! Now they had the problem of getting the rabbit down.

In his eagerness to meet the star Johnny forgot he hated heights. Now, when it dawned on him how high up he was, he was terrified. He would not budge and clung desperately to his branch.

He began to wish that he had never seen the star and fallen in love with her. He was frozen with fear and had no idea how to get down.

There was no alternative. Desperate measures had to be used to get Johnny down to the ground again.

Together the rabbits and squirrels gave Johnny a mighty push and he fell into the net spread under the tree.

Johnny fainted with the shock.

For many long days Johnny was delirious but Florence, his childhood friend, watched over him tenderly.

Florence had always loved Johnny.

When at last Johnny opened his eyes again, it was Florence he saw. How pretty she was! She was so pretty and so kind that Johnny soon forgot his star. He hardly ever thought to look at the sky anymore.

Florence and Johnny Rabbit got married. What a wedding! All the animals of the forest were invited. It was as though the sky was celebrating with them—for high in the heavens danced Johnny's star, the star of happiness.

The Puppy and the Boy

'What a lovable rascal that little Tom Thumb is. It's because he's so small that I called him that. He's really funny, with bright eyes and a tail that's much too long! He's a rascal with a heart of gold. If only he weren't so small and different from my other children. He's the only one with smooth fur and a tan and white coat. And that long, long tail that he wags all the time.'

That was how Mother Dog talked about her smallest son. But although he was small, Tom Thumb was full of adventure. As soon as his mother dozed off, he was off on a voyage of discovery.

Some days Tom Thumb would bound around the garden with his brothers and sisters. He was the most mischievous puppy of the litter. He would hide and jump out at them, chase them and snatch at the ball they were playing with. Other days he would stand by the gate, looking out at the people passing by. Sometimes he would pretend to be a fierce guard dog and would bark loudly when the milkman came near. Other

34

times he would make friends with the children who stopped to pat him, attracted by his friendly face and wagging tail.

Tom Thumb's world was full of so many wonders! This particular day he had heard that his young master was ill and would be in bed for many long months. Tom Thumb decided to get to know him for he had no idea what sick children looked like. He decided to start his search. Slipping through the half-open front door he reached the staircase. What a climb followed! How high the stars were! Using his back legs as a spring, Tom started the ascent.

Climbing was tough work, he decided. Many times he stopped to rest, and wondered whether it would not be better to roll back down again. But his curiosity to see the ill young boy got the better of him.

He eventually arrived, breathless, on the landing. Collecting his thoughts, he poked his head round the door of the bedroom. The young master, Peter, was lying there, pale and still, gazing out of the open window overlooking the garden. He was probably remembering that once he had run about there happily with his friends.

A lump came to Tom Thumb's throat. How sad it was to see Peter lying there helpless. Perhaps Tom Thumb could make him smile again.

First of all, Tom Thumb went about introducing himself by barking softly. The startled child looked down at the ball of fur beside the bed. Shyly, Tom Thumb came closer and tried to get himself up on to the bed. Climbing the steep wall of sheet was quite a venture! Many times he fell back, stunned, on to the floor! Finally Peter managed to grab him by the tail. He pulled him up on to the bed in front of him. Tom Thumb licked Peter's hand, and then cocked his head shyly at him.

Peter smiled and gently stroked Tom Thumb behind the ears. And that is how they made friends.

The friendship blossomed quickly and soon Peter was feeling pleasantly sleepy. In no time at all they both dozed off happily, Peter hugging Tom Thumb, who had nestled his head on his master's shoulder.

When Peter's mother came upon the touching scene, she quietly closed the door and left the puppy and the boy to sleep undisturbed.

From that day on they were the greatest of friends. Peter began to grow stronger, and was soon well enough to play in the garden again with his friends—and Tom Thumb.

Nellie and Fanta

Nellie and Fanta, two baby elephants, went down to the river to bathe.

Fanta dipped his trunk into the water, but quickly pulled it out again. 'Ugh!' he said. 'It's too warm! We need some rain to cool the river down.'

Preferring the shade of a tree to the sunshine, Fanta lay down under the branches.

The big lazybones was asleep in seconds.

Nellie pulled Fanta's tail, but he went on sleeping.

She rushed to the water and sprayed him all over.

Fanta finally condescended to open one eye. 'Let me sleep,' he growled, looking grumpy.

'I thought we had come to have fun!' said Nellie irritably.

'The water in the river made me

change my mind. Besides, it's too hot to play. Come and have a rest instead. We'll go for a walk afterwards,' yawned Fanta.

They both settled down in the long grass and were soon asleep.

Meanwhile, Dahlia, their mother, opened her eyes. 'Nellie! Fanta! Where are you? It's bath-time.'

But the call went unanswered.

'I must have been asleep a long time,' she said to herself, 'it's four o'clock by the sun.'

Very worried, Dahlia woke Mambo, the father of the two young elephants.

'What's the matter?' he grumbled. 'Why did you wake me?'

'The children have gone,' wailed Dahlia.

At these words, Mambo shook his great bulk and started to bellow. 'Dahlia, you fell asleep again,' he scolded, 'perhaps the children have fallen into a trap . . .'

'Yes, I did sleep for ages,' the elephant cried.

'Don't cry, Dahlia. They can't be very far. We'll find them.'

After searching for several hours the parents came across their two children, sleeping under a tree next to the river. What a hot day it was.

Tired after their search Dahlia and Mambo flopped down beside Nellie and Fanta.

Mambo was soon snoring but Dahlia, who had learnt her lesson, kept one eye on the mischievous children.

The Legend of the Plover and the Crocodile

The crocodile and the plover were old friends. The plover was never frightened to hop into the crocodile's mouth, and here is the reason why.

Once upon a time, the crocodiles of the world used to brush their teeth. They used an enormous oval brush which they cut from a tree called the toothbrush tree, which was very bountiful. It produced lots of toothbrushes. It was very useful and the crocodiles could make new toothbrushes as often as they liked. This they did very often, for they loved brushing their teeth. They liked to scrub them till they shone as white as snow. Then they would lean over and grin at their reflection in the water, admiring the way their teeth flashed in the sunlight.

And so the crocodiles were quite content. Until, one day, the planet was transformed and the tree disappeared for ever.

The crocodiles, on the other hand, stayed. Then they found themselves in quite a predicament. Crocodiles, you see, needed good strong teeth to chew their food. But how could they keep their teeth strong and healthy without cleaning them?

Soon it was a disaster. The crocodile's teeth went bad, and so many fell out they ended up eating gruel. It was no joke. The old crocodiles put up with it, but the young ones could not stand living that way, especially when they were very hungry.

One young crocodile called Charlie, a charming crocodile indeed, had made friends with a kind little bird called a plover.

The plover used to perch on his back to cross the river, or to bask in the sun when Charlie was lying on the beach.

One fine morning Charlie groaned, 'I've got a toothache. Ouch.'

'Let me have a look,' offered the plover.

Charlie didn't need to be asked twice, and quickly opened his mouth.

The plover walked around inside Charlie's mouth and inspected every tooth. 'I'm going to clean your teeth so they won't hurt any more.'

And that's exactly what he did. He made himself into a kind of toothbrush, using his pointed beak to pick out all the dirt that had lodged in poor Charlie's gums.

'That's fantastic,' said the crocodile when the job was done. 'It doesn't hurt at all now.'

Charlie rolled over and looked at his reflection in the water. His teeth looked nearly as good as teeth used to, in the days of the toothbrush tree.

Charlie told all his brothers, sisters and friends about his discovery. Straight away all the crocodiles asked the plovers to help them out and this was the beginning of a beautiful and lasting friendship.

Maisie and the Bean

Once upon a time there was a beanstalk growing in a neglected, overgrown garden. It was dying of thirst that very dry July.

In a nearby house lived Maisie, the white mouse, who spent all her days in a cage. Maisie decided to run away, and took refuge underneath the drooping leaves of the beanstalk. In the light of morning Maisie saw how thirsty the plant was, and watered it.

The beanstalk started to revive, and that same evening the mouse watered it again. Then, her duty done, she fell asleep.

The mouse did not know that she was carrying a powerful substance on her feet that made plants grow, so she was astounded the next morning to see the beanstalk stretching up to the sky.

Maisie thought of all the things she would be able to see from the top of the beanstalk, and decided to climb up the thick plant.

After a while Maisie felt tired. The beanstalk seemed to be neverending, and she started to feel giddy.

The bean went on growing and after a while deposited Maisie on a planet inhabited by white beans and blue mice.

Maisie was immediately proclaimed queen of the blue mice, and the bean became chief of the white beans.

The green bean got thicker and thicker, and turned into a tree which shaded the planet. As for Maisie, she lived perfectly happily in her new world.

A Wonderful Surprise

'Remember to stay in the shelter, darlings,' said Mummy Beaver to her children. 'I'm going to help your father build our new home.'

'Good-bye, Mummy,' replied the little beavers, falling asleep again with their noses between their front paws. It was so comfy in the soft bed and ever so warm.

But the Spring sun in the woods soon tempted them outside.

'What shall we play,' asked Nicky, the youngest. 'Shall we play hide-and-seek? Or tag? Or cops and robbers?'

'I've got an idea,' replied Basil, the eldest.

'You never want to do what I say,' said Nicky, quite hurt.

And it was quite true. The others never took Nicky seriously, or indeed listened to what he had to say. That was the penalty of being the youngest.

'I've got a *very* good idea,' said Basil again.

'Quick, tell us,' said Wiggle, the middle beaver, so named because of

the way she wiggled her tail.

'What if we made a little beaver den for ourselves?' was Basil's suggestion.

'Oh! That's too difficult!' Nicky protested.

'No it isn't,' Basil assured him. 'You'll see. I'm big, and I know how to do it. I've already helped Daddy. Come on, let's go down the river. We'll make our very own dam!'

Full of enthusiasm, the three beavers rushed off. What fun! To build a proper den!

Basil swam ahead and studied the banks. 'Here,' he said, 'this will do well. Let's start with the dam.'

'Yes, yes,' cried the others, 'the dam, the dam!' They felt very excited and grown up.

'Come on, we'll chop down this birch tree together.'

'Oh, let's chop a tree each, Basil,' Wiggle cried.

It was agreed, and the three beavers set upon three young trees.

Suddenly Basil noticed what Nicky was up to.

'Hey! Nicky, you clown, gnaw on the side of the tree so that it falls into the river!'

Furious at being called a clown, Nicky lay down at the foot of the birch and sulked.

'Blow the dam!' thought Nicky aloud. 'As I'm such a clown I won't do another thing! No. Not a thing. I'll be able to sleep, dream, go for a walk and have fun. So there.'

'Nicky, it was only a joke,' said Basil, 'you've been working well. I'll help you, come on.'

Nicky got up slowly and followed Basil.

Two sets of beaver teeth bit into the wood.

'Watch out, Nicky,' cried Wiggle. 'The tree is coming down. Come over here.'

Crack! Crash! And the tree had fallen right where Basil said it would.

'Well done, Nicky. And now you must cut it into pieces.'

Nicky worked with enthusiasm

and soon had prepared a big pile of logs. By evening the dam was finished. It had intertwined branches and mud that Wiggle had smoothed out with her wide tail.

'How well we've worked,' cried Nicky, admiring his handiwork.

The young beavers made their way home slowly, for they were very tired.

When they got back to their den under the water, the beavers found their worried parents already there.

'You didn't see any otters or foxes?' asked Mummy Beaver anxiously.

'No, Mummy, we've been working too hard,' cried Nicky.

Basil pinched his leg warningly. Nicky, the chatterbox, understood immediately that he mustn't give away their secret, and said, 'We've been working . . . at . . . playing.'

'You don't even know what you're saying,' Mummy replied. 'You are too tired from running and jumping. Into bed with you. Good-night children.'

On the following days, the beavers carried on building their hut with bits of wood, stones and mud. Nicky intertwined the branches, while Basil and Wiggle filled in the gaps with mud or cut down other birch trees.

The room was almost ready, with a very soft grassy bed, when all at once Nicky turned and shouted, 'The otter! The otter!'

Basil rushed along the tunnel under the hut and caught sight of a flat head with long whiskers just showing above the water. The otter swam without a sound, trying to catch them unawares.

Basil and Wiggle struggled with the otter which dived and disappeared under the floating weeds.

'Well done, Nicky. You are a good lookout!' said Basil. 'I was quite scared for a moment.'

'So was I,' confessed Nicky, still trembling, but proud that Basil was congratulating him.

'I hope that we have frightened the otter so much that she won't come back,' added Wiggle.

Finally, after some days, the little beavers were able to ask their parents to see the surprise.

'You must both come,' Nicky insisted.

'They have been so good just lately,' said Mummy Beaver to her husband. 'I can't wait to see what they have been up to! I can't think how they have been spending their time all day. I hope they haven't been up to any foolishness!'

She looked at the row of excited faces in front of her and smiled.

'Well, we'll see tomorrow,' Daddy Beaver answered calmly. 'In the meantime, it's bed for me. I'm awfully tired.'

Nicky was so impatient that he woke up early and made a lot of noise to let everyone know that it was time to get up.

'Well,' said Daddy Beaver finally, 'and where is your surprise, children?'

'You will have to come down the river with us,' they chorused.

'All right, let's all go together.'

What fun it was to swim together in the clear water which reflected the sun, and to hear the birds singing perched in the birch trees.

'This is our den,' said Nicky finally, pointing proudly.

'That's a good joke!' Daddy replied. 'Who lives here?'

'But it *is* our own den,' said Nicky. 'We built it ourselves.' And the others assured their parents that Nicky was telling the truth, that this was their surprise.

In amazement, Daddy and Mummy went into the hut and said, 'Well done children! This is a real surprise! Now we know you'll be able to look after yourselves in future.'

45

Snowy the Polar Bear Cub

On the big frozen ice-bank lived Snowy, the little white polar bear, with his parents and his friends the penguins.

He had so much fun sliding on the frozen snow!

'Be careful, Snowy, time to hide,' said Daddy Bear. 'Here come the hunters!'

Snowy knew what to do and rolled himself into a little ball in the snow and closed his eyes, making it difficult for the hunters to see him.

'It's all right now,' said Snowy's mother. 'They've gone.'

Then Snowy's father called, 'Snowy, come and fish for a salmon.'

Snowy had a feast, then returned to Mother Bear and gave her a fish.

'Oh!' cried the bear cub, suddenly pointing. 'I would like to go over there all alone, far far away, to see the edge of the sky.'

'When spring comes, my little Snowy,' said Mummy Bear, 'we will teach you to swim!'

Snowy listened but he didn't know what spring was—and it sounded a long way off.

The bear cub set off happily to

explore towards the faint sunlight.

But he went too far and didn't hear his mother calling, 'Snowy! Snowy!'

Only the seagulls answered: 'The white bear cub has gone to the sea.'

Mother Bear ran as fast as she could. Suddenly she heard a cracking sound. An iceberg had broken away from the ice-bank and was slipping far away, carried off by the tide. On the iceberg a little bear cowered all alone.

Splash! Mummy Bear dived in and swam after the iceberg, which was drifting even further away. 'Snowy, Snowy! Jump into the water and swim with me!'

'But I don't know how, Mummy,' wailed the bear. 'I'm frightened.'

'Go on, jump quickly. Then do as I do. Swim, swim, move your legs—again, again! There, that's good, Snowy. I'm right beside you.'

So it was that Snowy, the adventurous bear cub, got back to the ice-bank, to his Daddy and his friends the penguins and the seals.

What a clever little polar bear cub.

The Two Kangaroos

Before humans appeared on this earth, two kangaroos lived with the other animals.

They were very sweet and all white, which made the other animals a little jealous. Only the ermine thought she was as white as they were and had no bad feelings.

One fine morning the older kangaroo, who was called Kango, said to his brother: 'Joey, I feel like playing but I don't know what to play.'

Joey thought about it and replied, 'Let's jump!'

'That's not very interesting,' said Kango, shrugging his shoulders.

'Let's jump to see who can go the highest,' said Joey. 'We've never tried that before.

'I can jump the highest,' said Kango, very sure of himself. 'Watch!'

And he leapt higher and higher—so high that he went through a grey cloud that was passing overhead.

The cloud frowned.

'I'm sorry,' said Kango. 'I've jumped higher than I thought. 'I'll go down again.'

But when he looked down and saw how far away the ground was he felt giddy and shut his eyes in fright.

The cloud started shaking with laughter and the young kangaroo could not keep his balance. He quickly tore off strips of cloud to make the long descent.

The cloud was very cross. Kango hurried down the ladder back to earth.

Suddenly the cloud was in a good mood again and went on its way, laughing to itself.

Kango was surprised, and wondered why the cloud was laughing so much. He found out two minutes later when Joey saw him.

'You jumped very well,' he said, 'but you've gone all grey!'

Kango was covered in a sort of cloudy grey dust. He tried in vain to brush it off but in the end he had to accept that this was the way he was going to stay.

'You look magnificent,' said all the animals . . . and they meant it.

Joey was now very jealous of his brother. The wolf, who was his best friend, told him that it was wicked to have such feelings.

49

But they were not fooled and they decided to keep watch one night to see what Joey was up to.

The kangaroo managed to jump very high that night. He did not even see the day break. It made the sun laugh loudly, and it beamed a little red ray which landed in Joey's fur. He was astounded to find himself red all over.

The animals all laughed and clapped.

That is how today there are grey kangaroos and red kangaroos.

'I know,' admitted Joey, 'and I'm ashamed of myself.'

But still, more than anything, Joey wanted to be able to reach a grey cloud. So he trained every night in secret and managed to jump quite high.

Unfortunately Joey did not meet any clouds and he was getting tired— so tired that he slept all day long.

'I just can't sleep at night,' he told the other animals when they started asking questions.

50

Living Free

Samantha, the little mole, was always sad because she never ever saw the sun.

It was true she lived in a beautiful cave, with soft carpets and cushions and with furniture gleaming from so much polishing, yet she had no joy in her heart. She was alone and lonely. It was no good being surrounded by beautiful things when there was no one to share in the pleasure of them.

One summer morning, tired of being so cautious, and of listening to the advice that all the members of her family had heaped upon her all her life, Miss Samantha Mole, wearing her prettiest muslin dress, opened the trap door that separated her from the outside world and ventured out to face the universe.

Her knees were knocking with fright but she convinced herself, 'Danger, and even death, are better than that dull existence!'

At first the sun blinded her, but it soon warmed her chilled bones and

Samantha, full of sweet well-being, wandered here and there. She went up to the big trees, followed a butterfly's flight, listened with rapture to the happy singing of the birds and settled down comfortably on the bank of a river.

She had never felt such deep contentment in her life before.

'How beautiful nature is!' she exclaimed aloud.

'Hello!' cried a fish, popping his head out of the water. 'How do you do, madam! My name is George!'

Startled, Samantha leaped upwards. She hadn't been expecting company so loud or so soon!

'Don't run away,' scolded George. 'How can you be frightened of me, sentenced as I am to a life under the water!'

'What about me?' Samantha retorted. 'I was sentenced to live a life underground.' And she sighed as she remembered how dull her life usually was.

'Well, you're not there now, I see,' said George pompously, 'so you can hardly compare that with my lot . . .'

Suddenly Samantha realised how lucky she was. It was true that she could survive out of her underground world whereas George would die out of the water. She suddenly realised how selfish she had been in the past. She had felt sorry for herself, but had never paused to think that some creatures might be even worse off than she was.

With tears in her eyes, she cried, 'Poor George! I will come every day to keep you company.'

So it was that one often saw Samantha, the little mole, visiting her friend George and telling him all about the outside world. And George became a happy fish. Hearing the news every day meant he never felt such a strong desire to leave the water again.

52

The Silly Duckling

'Everyone into the water!' Mother Duck ordered her seven little ones. 'And keep close behind me!'

Proudly, she straightened her neck and led them to a spot where the reeds were so high that they would be hidden. For young ducks are beset by many dangers!

Dracko, the smallest duckling, and the most mischievous, was always being told, 'Don't hang around at the back all the time!'

'I wish I could hurry up and be a duck!' he sighed.

And the ducklings did grow into ducks who learned to fly. But Mother Duck kept up her warnings to Dracko.

Mrs Frog, coming out of the water, caught sight of them: 'Ugh,' she said, 'seven more greedy frog-eating ducks!' Then she ran away in leaps and bounds, taking her family with her.

'Oh ho!' said Dracko, spotting them. 'Frog! They would make a nice change of diet!'

Ready for anything, he followed them. But a sparrow-hawk swept down towards the duck.

Mrs Frog, seeing the bird of prey, called, 'Silly duck! Leave the frogs alone and look up! You are about to be carried off by the hawk!'

'Thank you, Mrs Frog. It would have served me right!' said Dracko gratefully. 'I hope I can help you one day.'

'You can do something for me. Eat something other than frogs!'

'Yes, I promise, I will tell all my family too,' promised Dracko.

How lovely to be all together again! But Dracko was still shaking. Shame-faced, he told his story and of his promise to the frogs.

The ducks swore they would never again eat the friendly frogs!

The Racoon and the Indian Boy

Woopy was a little Indian boy who lived with his parents in a village of tents on the edge of the forest.

Like all Indian boys, Woopy accompanied his father each day on fishing and hunting expeditions, because he, too, had to learn to use a bow and arrow. Often Woopy, who had a very kind heart, carried up the heavy buckets full of fresh water that his mother needed for the housework and cooking. He had learnt to build a hut out of branches, which a lost hunter could use as a shelter in bad weather, and also the art of smoking long strips of meat over a wood fire was no secret to him any more.

In other words, Woopy was growing up fast, and his parents were proud of him.

One morning, as he was fishing alone on board his little canoe, Woopy saw, wedged in between the mangrove roots, a ball of fur, moaning and shivering with cold. Using his paddle, Woopy pulled towards him a strange animal which looked tiny in its blood-stained fur. He picked it up in both hands and was surprised to find that it hardly weighed a thing. Woopy quickly set off for home with his find nestled warmly against his chest.

When he got home he showed it to his parents, who showed immediate interest.

'It's a baby racoon,' said his father, 'look at the brown rings round his eyes.'

Woopy's mother was sympathetic and kindly warmed up some milk and dressed the animal's wound. Soon the racoon was sleeping soundly with a full tummy.

The nights were cool, so Woopy slipped his little charge under his

55

own fur coverlet. And before he fell asleep, had named his new friend Fluff.

Fluff recovered quickly. His eyes, which were as black as liquorice, regained their sparkle, and a shine returned to his fur. Fluff's pretty beige and brown tail was as silky as could be.

Perched on Woopy's shoulder, Fluff was soon taking part in all Woopy's outings. Often the Indian boy would offer the young racoon some of the fish he caught. It amused him very much to see Fluff soaking, washing, rubbing and scratching the food before he would eat it.

Some time later, the women of the village got together and complained to the witch doctor about the exploits of a mysterious burglar.

The burglar had stolen a great number of sugarloaves, and also the precious salt and flour which had been carefully stored in a locked hut.

There was great indignation because the harsh Canadian winter was on its way and food was precious. It was decided to keep guard on the hut, but in spite of the watchful rounds, the thief went undiscovered. Eventually it was Woopy's turn for guard duty. Imagine his surprise when, as the new moon lit up the clearing, he saw Fluff slip between two logs and into the larder.

Fluff soon reappeared, clutching a sugarloaf to his chest, and took the path which led to the river. Woopy followed him, hiding as best he could. When he got to the water's edge, the little racoon, faithful to the customs of his race, soaked, rubbed and washed his booty. So much so, that when he was ready to taste it greedily, all that was left was a little sticky paste stuck to his paws, which he licked off, looking very disappointed. Woopy tried hard not to laugh.

Quite undaunted, Fluff set off on a new foray and before Woopy could intervene, the little racoon was back at work, scrubbing a block of rock-salt which underwent the same fate and soon melted under the vigorous little paws. But what a face Fluff pulled when, greedy as ever, he started to lick his sticky fur! Woopy intervened, and seized Fluff round the waist. Fluff, quite indignant, could not understand the reproaches that were heaped upon him. He had not realised he was doing anything wrong.

'You must let the racoon go,' the Witch Doctor wisely advised a tearful Woopy. 'He is grown up now and belongs with his brothers. Besides, we could not feed him with the harsh winter that is coming. He will be happier among his own kind, for he had to learn to survive according to the laws of nature. Take your canoe and leave him at the bend of the river, near the birch forest where you first found him. There is a whole colony of racoons there.'

Woopy was very sad at the thought of being parted from his little friend, but the words of the Witch Doctor were wise advice. It was so hard to survive in the middle of winter that,

57

at the Indian camp, every mouthful of food counted.

So the little Indian made the journey down the big river one last time, carrying Fluff in his pretty canoe.

Woopy landed on the bank near a forest of birch trees, whose leaves were already turning yellow in the autumn sun. He hugged his friend one last time, then put him on to dry land and quickly pushed away from the bank.

At first Fluff was surprised and started to protest in his own language, hopping up and down. Then he caught sight of another racoon picking juicy berries under a hedge, and he rushed off to play with him.

Woopy watched for a while then Fluff turned towards him and waved. Woopy waved back and Fluff disappeared into the bushes chattering to his new friend with delight. He had found his place again among his own kind.

Woopy sighed. Many tasks awaited him . . . the time for games was over.

Journey to the Moon

Tomkin and Catkin, two sweet kittens, were having a marvellous time jumping off the top of a hay-stack. They were using an old umbrella they had found at the back of the attic as a parachute, when who should pass by but Millie, a proud but very timid mouse.

'Let's ask her to play with us,' the two pals giggled into their whiskers.

'It depends on the game,' the mouse cautiously answered when asked.

'It's great fun! Come, you'll see how funny it is!'

Millie felt obliged to accept, so as not to look like a coward.

All went well, and the three new friends were enjoying themselves.

Even Millie began to like the game which took her completely out of her familiar world.

Intent as they were on their game, the three friends did not notice that it was getting dark and the wind was rising.

The umbrella was caught suddenly in a gust and turned upside down. Tomkin, Catkin and Millie were tumbled inside it and carried through the air. They shouted very loud but no one heard them.

Buffeted by the wind and carried along by its whims, they finally landed on the moon.

What a wonderful surprise for Millie! As she looked about her she saw the moon was made of cheese, and mice love cheese.

'Mm! What a feast I'm going to have,' she said to her two friends, who looked anything but pleased.

Millie immediately started to nibble at the cheese, and then ate so much that there was none left and the three friends plummeted down to earth!

The two kittens were very cross because with no moon, the nights were dark and sad. They decided, with the help of the stars, to build another moon out of patches of light instead of cheese.

They got to work on this difficult plan. Each star contributed a drop of light, until soon they had made a bright, round moon.

Tomkin and Catkin were happy to see the moon shining again, but Millie had to be taught a lesson!

The little mouse had already been punished, for her tummy hurt so much that she had to take lots of castor oil. Ugh! It was horrid!

In spite of Millie's suffering, Tomkin and Catkin could not forgive her and chased her every time they saw her.

That is why mice always run away from cats!

The Legend of the Robin

In the great jade forest, the gentle Crown Prince sat on the green moss and cried. He called desperately for help, since he was lost and hurt, and far from his marble palace. The first to hear his calls of distress was a white dove, who was hovering overhead.

'Dove, my sweet, take this handkerchief to my father, so that he will come on his horse to fetch me.'

The dove looked very affronted at this.

'And ruin my snow white feathers on such a long journey? You must be joking!' she said scornfully.

And without further ado she flew off in a flurry of silvery wings.

A pair of blackbirds all dressed in black were the next to stop near the Prince. He gazed up at them and entreated wearily,

'Friends, sweet friends, go and give this handkerchief to my father, the King, to let him know that his son is lost in the heart of the emerald forest!'

'Sweet Prince, we are in a hurry because we must build our nests before the leaves turn yellow.' And they flew off, leaving the Prince to his misery.

A blue tit came next to the Prince.

'You who are like quicksilver, fly with all speed to my father to tell him that his child is frightened so far from home.'

'Almost as soon as I leave you, little Prince, I will have forgotten that I ever met you. That is how I am, empty-headed!'

And she flew off, fragile and care-free, into the blue sky.

Just as the Prince was losing all hope of being saved, a little brown bird, as plain as could be, landed on the Prince's hand. He was a warm-hearted bird and felt sad to see the Prince so unhappy and ill. He just had to do something to save the gentle blond Prince. He seized the embroidered blood-stained hand-kerchief and set off to fly to the castle.

It was a very long journey for such a tiny bird! He felt his strength ebbing away. Finally he reached the castle, and with exhaustion fell at

the feet of the King, who was watching from the battlements with the Queen for the return of the fair Prince.

The King quickly picked up the little bird and put him into the Queen's hands, so that she could comfort him. Then, the embroidered handkerchief against his heart, he set off to search for his son. And so the little Prince of the Magic Kingdom was rescued and he rewarded his kind-hearted friend. He dubbed the little brown bird the Knight of the Rose. Instead of giving him a medal for this great honour, he decorated the bird's breast with a scarlet rose. He looked magnificent with his breast blazing like the colour of a fiery sun.

The little bird was bursting with pride at the honour. He had not helped the prince for personal glory.

So it was that the bird became the robin red-breast and as a token of his gratitude to the bird, the King made him for ever the true friend of the country people and the townspeople.

The Queen, for her part, wished to protect the robin from his mortal enemy the winter. So she made sure that he would always be helped by humans. That is why, when winter comes, the little robin red-breast comes right up to the houses, and will tap boldly on the windows for food. This way the robin can be sure of surviving until the next spring.

To this very day, the pact between Man and the robin has never been broken. Over the centuries the robin, flower of our gardens, has come to understand that he has nothing to fear from Man.

Pretty little red-breast, you light up our dull grey days, and we will go on protecting you. In this way, you will survive, and the changing seasons to give us even greater pleasure. You will always be the spark of life of our white winters.

Pony of the Sea

Jinx loved his island where he grazed the grass and the thistles, and tasted the flowering heather. But he was also drawn to the sea.

'If I had a little boat,' Jinx, the colt, daydreamed, 'I could go to the island of the lighthouse and bring back pink shrimps, green lobsters and shiny fishes.'

One day there was a strong tide, and the sea had ebbed far away showing Jinx sand that he had never seen before. The sea seemed so distant that Jinx could hardly see the fishermen with their lobster pots.

Jinx leaped through the sand, then from rock to rock.

Before long Jinx found himself at the place that he had admired from afar.

'My little island! My little island! At last!' cried Jinx and he rested in the shadow of the lighthouse.

Jinx was so happy that he did not notice that the tide had turned and was slowly coming in again.

Evening fell and the purple sea encircled the island with a ruff of foam and growled between the rocks.

'Crafty old sea!' cried Jinx. 'It has covered the path home.'

Jinx galloped in the wind on the

lighthouse island, which was getting smaller and smaller.

He felt a sense of excitement and freedom, of a dream come true. Looking back over the way he had come, now covered with water, he felt he had begun a new life.

Night came and the starry sky looked enormous.

'Oh,' said Jinx, 'I would like to run among the stars! It must be wonderful!' And he lay down and wondered how he could reach the sky.

The high, black rocks of his island home looked like wild animals, but Jinx was not frightened. It was a joy for the young colt to spend the night by starlight on his very own island!

He hadn't even given a thought to his mother, who was looking every-where for him.

His father reassured her and said, 'Your colt will be back tomorrow when the sea has gone out. Right now he must be sleeping.'

It was true. Jinx had fallen asleep next to the lighthouse watched over by the stars and surrounded by his beloved sea.

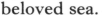

The Three Fishes

Flip! Flop! Arabella and Phoebe, two magnificent Japanese fishes with huge transparent glowing fins like the veils of an oriental dancing girl, were lying in a puddle of water near the living-room sofa.

The adventure had turned out badly, in spite of plans carefully worked out over several days under the wry gaze of Gilbert, the old goldfish.

'Ah! To see a change of scene! To be like the birds in the garden, what a dream!' One attempt succeeded another, as Gilbert watched frowning. He was irritated by the jerky arabesques, and the toing and froing of his cousins, as they tried to jump.

Today was the big day. The two fish took off from the bottom of the aquarium. They swam hard, rose by beating the air desperately with their shimmering fins, and flew out. But to where? They plunged down to the floor where they could be seen by an amused Gilbert.

'Who will find us? We will die without water,' they wailed.

Later, the young owner of the three fish went to feed her charges and was surprised to see Gilbert all alone. She looked around for them and started to cry. The goldfish, forgetting his grudge, summoned all his strength. He reared himself up and jumped up to join the two Japanese fish.

Valerie saw where he fell and noticed the others. Beside herself with joy she picked up the fishes, more dead than alive, in her hands.

The three fish soon became the best friends in the world again.

Barnaby and Caroline

Barnaby, a reddish-brown donkey, with fur the warm colour of squirrel fur, had a special friend. She was a little girl, seven years old, called Caroline, who lived next door to his farm.

'Come along, Barnaby. Let's go somewhere nice together.'

'Get on my back, Caroline. I will carry you.'

So the two friends left the farm that fine summer's morning to go to the seaside.

The dew was shining on the green grass and the hawthorn smelled sweet as they passed.

'Hello, hello,' said the foals.

'Have a good journey!' chorused the calves.

'Have a nice day!' added the squirrels.

'I will bring you back some pretty shells,' Caroline promised.

Barnaby continued his journey along the lovely road towards the sea which he had never seen . . .

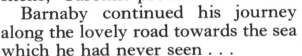

'What is the sea like?' he asked Caroline.

'You'll like it, I promise,' replied Caroline.

From time to time Barnaby tasted the sweet grass and the flowered thistles. The butterflies fluttered around Caroline, whilst the bright-winged dragonflies sought the coolness of the stream . . .

Caroline and Barnaby trotted along contentedly.

At last, the moment they had both waited for arrived, and they reached the sea.

'How big the sea is! And how beautiful,' cried Barnaby.

'We can walk in the water. It's not deep at the edge. Come on!' encouraged Caroline.

Barnaby had only paddled in a still pond before, and it was a new experience for him to feel the waves lapping against him.

The two friends played all day long in the waves. They played in the warm sand and built castles and forts. The sheep from the sandhills came along to help them.

Barnaby and Caroline were so

happy that they completely forgot the time.

When the red sun sank beneath the water and the sea turned first mauve and pink and then purple, they realised that the evening had arrived.

'Stay here with us,' offered the lambs. 'We have a big hut.'

'No, thank you,' Caroline replied politely, 'we must go home.'

On the deserted road, surrounded by darkness, the two friends set off on their journey through the sleeping countryside.

The silver stars twinkled down on them like thousands of diamonds in the night sky.

'How beautiful it is!' said Barnaby, stopping to admire the sight. Then he trotted along the path lit by the moon.

Barnaby and Caroline got slower and slower. Was it because they were tired from the sun and the journey? Of was it that they were afraid of being scolded? Or was it that they wanted to stay being happy for ever?

Tied to a rope in a dark corner of

the lonely stable, Barnaby had lost his appetite. His back hurt from so much beating. His gentle eyes were full of tears. He would never see his dear friend Caroline again.

Barnaby remembered that lovely day . . . the sunshine, the flowers, the butterflies and the birds. But most of all he remembered the great big sea and his friend Caroline.

Poor Barnaby. Poor brown donkey!

In the house next door, everyone was walking on tiptoe. Caroline was ill and had a high fever. She had spent too long in the hot summer sun. 'My friend, I want my friend Barnaby!' she cried over and over again.

'You must not upset her,' the doctor had warned. 'Whatever hap-pens, do not let her cry!'

Caroline's father disappeared down the flowered path and made for the farm. What could he say to the farmer?

Caroline awoke. What did she see?

Barnaby was lying there right next to the bed. He licked her hand softly and said, 'I will never leave you again, Caroline. Get better quickly.'

'Barnaby belongs to you now,' murmured her father. 'I bought him from the farmer.'

'Oh Daddy! You've made me the happiest girl in the world! You have given me back my friend Barnaby!'

They both went to the sea often after that, but never stayed out too late!

The Dog With No Master

It was Christmas Eve and a cold night. Caramel, the honey-coloured dog, sniffed along the edge of the pavement. He was all alone . . .

The people on the streets were rushing around, busily buying gifts. No one noticed Caramel, the lonely dog, the dog with no master.

Inside a warm house, Caramel saw the big Christmas tree glowing with lights.

'It's Christmas Eve!' the children were singing.

As Caramel looked in at the window he felt cold all over, especially inside his heart. Everyone had forgotten him . . .

Caramel heard the footsteps of a lone walker. 'Who's there?' he asked.

A shadow bent over him.

A hand stroked him gently.

'What's the matter, dog? Are you lost?' a voice asked.

'No, I'm just lonely,' replied Caramel.

The youngster looked at Caramel.

The dog looked up and licked the stranger. He had red hair which fell in front of his eyes.

'Do you want to be my friend?' asked the boy.

'Please,' replied Caramel.

So the two of them walked from

the lighted window together without looking back. They both suddenly felt happy. They would be lonely no longer; they had each other.

They walked for a long time in the dark, across the waste land where the wild grass was swaying in the cold wind.

Finally, they arrived at an old caravan. There Caramel and his friend found some comfort.

They huddled up to the stove.

'You can share my milk,' offered the boy, 'and tomorrow we will hunt for rabbit.'

Then they nestled up to each other on a pile of rags and fell asleep.

From that day on, the dog with no master and the little urchin were never parted.

They are happy together,
All through the springtime,
Jumping in the morn,
All through the summertime,
Running through the corn,
All through the wintertime,
Sliding on the snow,
And especially on Christmas Eve
As they love each other so.

The Little House of Friendship

Right at the top of the big oak tree, Simon the squirrel woke up in his nest carpeted with dry leaves and moss, and ran down the trunk.

'Spring is a long way off. Oh, I'd dearly love to hear the forest singing once more.'

'So would I,' replied Harry, the hedgehog.

'Listen,' suggested Simon thoughtfully. 'Let's build a friendship house for the poor birds who are frozen in the middle of the winter.'

Harry thought that this was a very good idea indeed. They would be of help to the birds, and would also make new friends.

Simon and Harry worked without a break.

They built a pretty log house with a big chimney.

They made nests with plaited twigs, down, moss, a little wool and a lot of love.

The dormouse and the weasel, the wild rabbit and the fieldmouse all helped too.

The birds sang and worked and worked and sang.

Simon and Harry looked at their house of friendship with pleasure.

With the first gusts of winter, the birds arrived: the greenfinches and

73

the red-breasts; the blue tits and the bullfinches; the larks and the doves; the wagtails, the warblers and the chaffinches.

Simon and Harry scoured the deserted pathways to find birds who had been overcome by cold in the freezing snow. They carried them back to the house and warmed them by the fire. They rubbed them down and put them in the soft nests.

Huddled in the warmth, the birds recovered fast. They sang their joy and thanks. The whole forest was singing in the house: it seemed like spring in the middle of winter.

But one night a storm raged in the forest. 'I'm going along the path,' declared Simon. 'On a night like this there are bound to be cold, tired birds in need of a home.'

'No,' said Harry, 'you are tired. Stay here. I'll go.'

'No, I'll go,' Simon insisted. 'You look after the fire.'

Simon didn't come back. Although Harry looked hard, the snow had covered his prints.

A squirrel lay as if dead. There was no movement except for the snow swirling all around. 'Well, well,' said the owl from the old mill who had been keeping watch from her attic window. 'I had better take a look.'

It was Simon, flat out on the frozen snow. She shook him but he didn't move.

The old owl realised that she couldn't carry the squirrel in by herself.

'Little ones, come and help me!' the owl called.

The young owls stretched out their velvety wings to carry the squirrel to the dusty mill where they rubbed him warm.

'Thank you,' said Simon gratefully. 'I feel better now. I must get home.'

'I'm coming with you,' the owl decided. 'You are not strong enough to make the journey by yourself.'

Simon arrived back with the owl, followed by all the birds who had been out looking for him.

'At last!' said the birds. 'If you knew how frightened we were!'

Simon settled down gratefully in the warm. Suddenly he realised he hadn't seen his old friend the hedgehog.

'Where is Harry?' asked Simon.

'Out looking for you, in spite of the storm.'

Finally, Harry came home all covered in snow and cried: 'Here you are after all! I am so happy!'

Simon warmed himself in front of the high flames and looked at the owl: 'You can't go off again in this weather,' he said.

'Well than,' suggested the owl. 'I will stay here and sing all night long, for spring will soon be back in the forest.'

It was not only the owl who wished to sing. All the birds of the house joined in.

The concert in the house of friendship was so full of joy and happiness that the shooting stars seemed to stop for a moment to listen to the sweet sounds.

The Proud Cockerel

Master Julius was so proud that he threw out his crop and preened himself. Master Julius the cockerel was going to be a father! Father to dozens of downy little chicks, because all the hens in the roost were laying.

The nests were full of eggs. Julius was beside himself with joy and vanity. There was no doubt that the farmer's wife would be thrilled and would give him some extra titbits.

He could just see himself ruling over a host of little hens who, in turn, would lay eggs. His descendants would fill the farmer's wallet when he went to sell them at the village fair. What a prospect!

Julius was impatient to let his friends know what a clever father he was. He covered the countryside in all directions excitedly telling his news. Sometimes exaggerating, sometimes telling one or two lies to the other cockerels who listened to him. They were dumbfounded, and a little jealous of his luck. His comb turned scarlet and quivered like a jelly, his eyes sparkled and his feathers fluffed up; he really did look grand.

Soon, there was not one roost in the neighbourhood that did not know about Julius becoming a father. Everyone was as impatient as he for the great day.

One morning, the farmyard was in a turmoil. Startled clucking and high-pitched chirping rose to a deafening din. The moment had come for the chicks to hatch out of their shells. Julius preferred to wait until it was all over before making his grand entrance in triumph. He want-

ed to wait until the mothers had calmed down and the children were asleep under their comforting wings.

After biding his time Julius got ready and smoothed his brilliant feathers one last time. He raised his spurs and, like a conqueror, entered the building.

Horror! Despair! Julius looked thunderstruck at his offspring. What had happened? He was distraught, but those stupid hens hadn't noticed a thing!

Among a few little golden-yellow balls, which he recognised as his children, were some awful grey creatures with flat beaks and webbed feet. There were others with rickety legs and piercing squeaks. Julius took refuge at the bottom of the garden, while his friends all laughed.

He did not realise that the farmer's wife had slipped some duck eggs, some turkey eggs and some guinea-fowl eggs under the broody hens.

Julius won't brag any more.

79

The Fox and the Hen

There was once a mischievous little fox called Brian and a wise hen called Sara. Sara was always kind and obliging, and was always the first to help any other creature in trouble.

Brian lived in the wood. Sara lived in the run at the edge of the farm.

One fine morning, Brian's mother said, 'Go and look for your food and don't forget that hens taste delicious.'

Brian bounded straight off to the hen run and hid himself in the bushes, waiting for the right moment to jump out and pounce on a hen.

It wasn't easy for Brian as Sara was guarding her companions carefully.

The little fox ran away crestfallen but tried again the following night.

He fared no better. The hens shrieked and defended themselves, leaving Brian with his hunger, which was growing all the time.

Sara comforted him, and taught him to eat eggs and feed himself without having to kill.

'Our mash is delicious,' she said. 'Come and share it with us.'

It was a good idea.

Brian was not hungry any more and Sara could sing all the time.

The Unripe Lolly

'How careless!' murmured William the hedgehog when he saw something lying on the steps that led to the house where the little girl lived.

He trotted closer. His spines were flat and his muzzle pointed as he sniffed the warm summer air. A pleasant sweet smell tickled his nostrils, and he gave thanks for the forgetfulness of his young friend. She often left titbits like that for him to enjoy.

William peered closer at the unexpected gift.

'It looks like an ice lolly,' he said to himself.

Indeed, it was an ice lolly. William had tasted them before, but they had been pink, orange or chocolate. This one was green, a pretty pale green.

The curious little snout sniffed furiously. It smelled all right, but what a funny colour it was!

William pondered for a long time before taking the stick of ice lolly. He carefully dragged it into the sunny garden. It was plain that the unusual colour meant that it was not ripe. The girl had obviously left the ice lolly there to ripen.

The hedgehog began to get impatient. He was very hot, and so was the sun, but still the ice lolly was as green as ever.

William decided to visit his friends while waiting for the warm rays of the sun to turn the lolly red.

On his way, he enjoyed the taste in his imagination and licked his lips. His eyes were round with pleasure, his nose quivered with delight and he could not help skipping and whistling.

All the animals of the farmyard heard about William's discovery.

They envied him because they

had never seen, let alone eaten, such delicacies. Their daily ration of cereals was appetising enough, but a little of something new would not have gone amiss!

They asked William wistfully what the lolly would be like to eat. And they listened so intently to his explanations that he realised they might like to taste it too.

William had a good heart and invited his companions to join in the party. 'Come along, my friends! You'll see, there is nothing more delicious, I promise you.'

The whole troop set off happily with William leading proudly.

The countryside echoed with quacking and cackling, as they all looked forward to the feast to come.

Suddenly the company stopped in its tracks. 'Here we are,' said William brightly to the others.

But all they could see in front of them was a little white stick!

Dumbfounded, William sadly realised that the ice had melted.

Dejected, the animals trooped back and the hedgehog swore that from now on, he would enjoy his finds straight away—ripe or unripe.

Midge Goes Swimming

Dusk was falling. The sun had cooled and turned the heavens pink. The tropical night would soon plunge the jungle into darkness.

All the animals were parched after their day in the hot sun, and had come to drink together. Hunter and quarry stood side by side.

Leona, the lioness, had brought her son Midge to the watering place for the first time. He bounded along carelessly despite the anxious warnings of his mother.

Leona was parched and lapped the refreshing water avidly, forgetting to keep an eye on her rascal of a son.

The river was low. Midge leaped on to the sandbanks above the surface of the water, then on to large smooth rocks. Without realising, he was getting further and further from the bank. He finally stopped on a big round rock, and looked around.

Suddenly the rock started to move. Hunk, the hippopotamus, had just finished his nap and was heading back to dry land. Wanting a last little swim before going back to the bank, he rolled over with relish in the calm water. Midge howled with terror and to avoid being crushed by the huge bulk jumped into the water. Midge could not swim. He struggled in the water, choking with fear, until he realised that his feet were on the bottom. He had had such a fright that he burst into tears.

'Is that you, Midge?' cried Hunk furiously. 'What do you think my back is . . . a canoe? You have deafened me with your wailing so please stop crying. My voice may be fierce but I am not cruel. Come along now I will take you back to your mother.'

The lion cub went back the way he came, only this time proudly perched on the back of his new friend. He had already forgotten about his misadventure and thought only of his triumphant return.

Celia Cricket Goes to Canada

Under the warm sun, Celia cricket was singing in her funny voice.

But it was so hot that she became very thirsty and flew to the round fountain in the sleepy little village to quench her thirst.

The shutters of all the houses were closed while everyone was having a nap or sipping cool drinks. Celia heard a man in a shop talking about a country called Canada.

'It must be lovely and cool,' thought Celia eagerly. 'I think I'll go there to live.'

She went to ask advice from her friend Penny.

'You will be too cold over there,' said sensible Penny. 'You won't be able to stand the weather.'

But Celia was stubborn. As she had made up her mind to go, nothing would stop her. And this she told Penny quite bluntly.

Penny, resigned to it, gave her a woollen shawl and some fluffy warm slippers that she had knitted. 'You will need them,' she said kindly.

Celia thanked her friend and made for the airport where she spied a woodcutter's suitcase.

'What luck!' thought Celia the cricket and slipped into the case.

The woodcutter's case was picked up and packed inside the plane with all the other luggage. No one had any idea that a little cricket was inside. She made herself a snug little bed inside the woodcutter's jumper, and settled down to enjoy herself.

Celia's great adventure began.

On the flight Celia felt a bit air-sick but she told herself that she would soon see the beautiful forests of Canada.

And it was that thought that got her through the bad moments.

When the woodcutter opened his case Celia hurriedly flew off and

found herself, filled with wonder, in the forest.

She hadn't gone two steps when the first animal she saw was a pretty squirrel eating a nut.

'What a strange creature!' he said aloud, dropping his nut in astonishment. And he went to tell his friends the beavers, who were building a dam.

The news spread quickly from mouth to ear, from beak to snout. An hour later, Celia, very happy and contented, answered all the questions that the animals asked her and the day went by quickly.

In the evening Celia wrapped the shawl around her shoulders and was grateful Penny had made it for her.

On the days that followed, Celia had great fun with her new friends exploring the forest and meeting the various animals.

It was as beautiful as she had

expected it to be, and more.

Then came the first wind of golden autumn, and with it a bad cold for Celia who went to bed with a high temperature.

Her friends looked after her with devotion. In her delirium, Celia cried out for warmth.

The beavers were very moved. They built a raft for her, and asked three racoons to take her as far as the port. There she could board a ship for home.

As soon as she was better, Celia thanked her friends and promised to come back the following summer. 'Canada is so beautiful!'

'We will get clothes ready for you, and bootees and a hat,' said the animals, rather sad to see her go.

Celia quickly got on to the raft and sailed towards the port. What tales she would have to tell when she got home!

Eddie's Trunk

Eddie was a good-looking elephant, with shiny hair and a very pleasant face. The only thing that wasn't quite right was his trunk, which was very tiny as far as elephant's trunks go. This caused Eddie much heartache.

Eddie's best friends were the birds who whistled happily when they saw him pass by, 'Eddie! There's Eddie!'

One day as he approached the nest of his special friends, the lovebirds, he heard someone crying and went to see what was wrong. Mrs Lovebird explained through her tears, 'Our little one has fallen into the river and there is no way to reach him.'

Eddie rushed to the river, where the little bird was struggling desperately in the cruel water. Eddie bent over the water and stretched his trunk as far as it would go. 'Catch hold of my trunk, little one!'

The bird perched on the improvised branch, and Eddie carried him back in triumph to the family nest.

From then on, Eddie was not ashamed—his now famous trunk had saved the life of the lovebird.

Polly and the Wolf

It was very cold. Snow was falling, the wind was raging in the forest and over the enormous plain.

The chilled birds fluffed up their feathers for warmth, while the other animals stayed safely inside their burrows or under shelter.

In her house near the forest, Polly was singing gaily in front of the fire where the flames crackled. She was snug and warm inside her sturdy little house. There were no draughts, the curtains were tightly drawn, and it was possible to forget the cold outside. She was happy and warm as she prepared the evening meal. How good the smell was.

Not far away roamed a young wolf, starving and cold. It was several days since he had anything to eat. The wolf came upon the house and knew he would not be welcomed by the humans. But his hunger made him bold.

Quietly at first, then louder, he howled outside little Polly's house.

'A wolf!' said the girl, who stopped singing at once.

Polly was a little afraid. Her parents were not there. What should she do?

'Hou! Hou!' howled the wolf again.

Polly looked out of the window. 'He seems very miserable,' she said. 'Perhaps he isn't a bad wolf.'

She opened the door a crack and a gust of wind pushed it open even further.

The wolf saw his chance and leaped into the middle of the room where he fell exhausted in front of the fire and closed his eyes.

'Well,' said Polly, 'you don't look very happy.'

She could see that he was too hungry and exhausted to be fierce, and she wasn't frightened of him.

She gave him food. It was what the wolf needed most and he devoured it hungrily. Then the beast licked her hands in gratitude and affection.

'We're going to be good friends,' said Polly knowingly. And not having the heart to send him outdoors again, she offered to let him share her room. The wolf settled on the soft carpet and was soon fast asleep.

From that moment on, a new life began for Polly and the wolf.

On fine days when the snow sparkled, they would go for walks.

Even Polly's parents, who had been nervous about Polly's choice of pet, grew fond of him.

When spring arrived at last it was time for the wolf to return to his family but Polly wasn't sad; she knew he would be back again in the first cold days of winter.

The Homesick Monkey

In the old harbour, not far from the boats, was a shop selling all sorts of animals. They were brought there from exotic lands by the sailors: beautiful birds; strange shaped fishes; and a little monkey.

Micky, the little monkey, locked in his cage, grew terribly bored. But, that night, when the old shopkeeper went to feed him, he did not shut the door of the cage properly. As soon as the old man's back was turned, Micky escaped.

In a few leaps, Micky reached the next street, and then the next town, until he finally reached a village where there was a big circus, sparkling with lights.

Micky was small and thin, and darted unnoticed through the crowds thronging at the box office. Passing by the cages and stalls where all sorts of wild animals were crowded, he hid in the corner of a huge tent.

How lovely everything was . . . the music, the lights, the elegant people.

Micky admired the magnificent horses with their heads adorned with splendid plumes and the elephants covered with sparkling ornaments. He was also impressed by the clever dogs dressed up in vivid costumes.

'How wonderful to be admired and applauded by thousands of delighted spectators,' thought Micky. He remembered how, in his native forest, he used to do much more

89

spectacular somersaults than the ones being performed in the circus. He felt the urge to leap into the ring and jump right to the top of the tent, to be applauded and admired by everyone. He felt that if he could do this he would at last be happy in this strange country.

But as the show wore on Micky noticed that the animals did not look any happier than the ones in the shop. He remembered too the cages and stalls he had passed on his way to the big top. Perhaps a circus life wasn't the life for him after all.

Suddenly, his mind made up, Micky found the exit and, noiseless and agile, he made for the deserted streets until he reached the harbour. There he found a boat leaving for Africa and managed to hide on the bridge. Tomorrow, when the ship had reached the open sea, he would go and scrounge some food from the sailors who were kind fellows. And in a week or two, he would be back in his homeland in the beautiful wild forest, where he could be free.

But Micky would never forget the sad faces of the animals he had left behind.

90

Pongo on Happy Island

One morning, Pongo, the penguin, was sitting on an enormous block of ice. He decided to let the waves carry him where ever they wished.

Spring had just arrived, and the penguins, the snow hares and the partridges were celebrating its return.

In the meantime, Pongo, suitably balanced, was drifting away.

'Where is he going?' the snow hares asked each other in surprise, for they had never known Pongo behave so oddly before.

'What is Pongo doing on that block of ice?' the astounded reindeer asked, shaking their antlers.

No one knew the answer to these questions, least of all Pongo. It was an adventure, that was all. It was a lovely, clear, warm day. Just the weather for drifting without a care in the world.

The sea carried the block of ice a long way and the warm, laughing sun was beginning to heat up. The ice was slowly melting but the little penguin did not notice. Then suddenly he realised that there was only room on the floating platform for his two webbed feet. 'I will have to jump into the water,' Pongo decided. So he leapt into the waves. He soon got tired and looked for something near-by which could carry him to an island he had glimpsed in the distance.

A tree-trunk, washed away by the current, provided an improvised raft. Pongo rowed as hard as he could, and reached the island where there were enormous trees, flowers, birds and rabbits. It was not at all like the place he had left behind him, so he decided to explore.

Pongo wandered about on the

island. 'What a funny bird!' the rabbits whispered to each other. Finally, a brave woodpecker asked Pongo kindly, 'What are you doing here?'

'I'm going round the world,' Pongo replied. 'But I don't know where I am at the moment.'

'You are on Happy Island,' a bird of paradise kindly told him.

'It's very pretty,' said Pongo approvingly. However, as he felt very hot, he asked for a little ice.

The rabbits opened their eyes wide and twitched their ears apologetically. 'We don't know what that is.'

'Never mind,' said Pongo resigned, 'perhaps you could fan me?'

He found it much too hot, so he mopped his brow with a handkerchief.

The rabbits made a fan out of large leaves and took it in turns to fan the penguin. Then they offered him some eggs, bananas and carrots to eat. Alas! Pongo did not eat such food. 'I only like fish,' he said, rather embarrassed. Pongo was beginning to realise that although this island was beautiful, he would have difficulty surviving on it. The rabbits found Pongo some fish and gave it to him.

Unfortunately, Pongo also did not like the taste of the fish which lived in that part of the sea, and the penguin had to think about leaving.

The rabbits were distraught. 'We could go and fetch you anything you want,' they offered.

'Please don't bother,' the penguin replied. 'I will only feel really well at home. The heat here tires me much too much.'

Indeed Pongo could only drag himself about. He had lost all the liveliness that he usually possessed.

The rabbits sympathised with the penguin's plight and set about building him a raft out of palm leaves.

'Have a good journey!' said the rabbits.

'Thank you, everybody,' Pongo replied, very moved.

There was a favourable wind which pushed the raft along so fast that Pongo soon reached his home again.

'There you are! Where have you been?' the snow partridge asked anxiously.

All the animals surrounded him, hardly believing their eyes. The hares, the reindeer, and his brother penguins came up.

'I'm dying of hunger.' Pongo confessed. He swallowed several fishes in one go and then recounted his adventure.

The hares waggled their long ears joyfully. 'What a wonderful journey!'

'Yes it was,' admitted Pongo, 'but I am very happy to be back.'

The Strange Rabbit Colony

Bunny, the wild rabbit, lived in the dunes. He played at night with his friends by the light of the moon under the starry sky.

One day he jumped out of his burrow to go and look for clover and wild thyme. He said 'good morning' to the seagulls and to the blue sky.

Bunny was the happiest of the wild rabbits playing on the sunny dune or nestling at the bottom of their sandpit.

What great races they used to have around the blue thistles!

All summer long, Bunny and his rabbit friends skipped around without a care in the world. Up early every day, they would find food together, rest together, and play together.

But the high winds of autumn made the reeds shiver and soon the hunters would arrive with their lively dogs.

'Take care, Bunny!' warned Mother Rabbit. 'Take care not to go out in daylight any more or the dogs will see you and the hunters will shoot you!'

But Bunny wanted to sniff the scent of the thyme, and nibble at the

94

last carrots in the fields near the marsh. He didn't want to stay at home all day.

Suddenly Bunny had an idea. 'I am going to build a little house just for me, the likes of which the hunters and the dogs have never seen before.'

His mother thought that this was a very strange idea and tried to dissuade Bunny. But he was very pleased with his plan and insisted on going ahead.

In a corner Bunny then found a slightly damaged blue plastic bucket. He rolled it down to the foot of the dune and followed it.

He placed the bucket in the hollow of the dune behind the big purple thistles, facing the sea.

What a lovely little house he had!

'Come and look, all of you, at my pretty little house!' cried Bunny with excitement. All his little rabbit friends came to see what Bunny had done, and were most impressed.

Bunny stocked up his store of thyme, rosemary, clover and grass. Early in the morning he hopped back into his house and watched where the hunters and the dogs were going and thumped out warnings to his friends.

'Find them, find them,' shouted the hunters. 'Come on, look harder. You must find them!'

The dogs scratched and sometimes went into the burrows but the rabbits had gone. Where could they be?

The hunters were furious—not a single rabbit caught. They couldn't understand it. The area was famous for its families of rabbits, but now there didn't seem to be one left anywhere!

Then one fine day, a very strange sight could be seen on the flowery dune.

If you looked carefully you could see a colony of rabbits racing under their yellow, blue and orange buckets hidden among the thistles and the weeds.

Bunny's friends had come to join him, and they loved their new homes.

95

In Pretty Wood

In the heart of Pretty Wood, the big trees sheltered the cottage where a little old man and his wife lived.

In the spring the little old man would hoe his garden and the birds would sing.

The old lady sowed tiny seeds against the cottage wall to blossom into bright flowers in the sunshine.

In the summer the old man and lady picked fruit and vegetables from the garden, and prepared their provisions of peas, beans and tomatoes. When the morning dew was fresh, the old man could be seen picking the best mushrooms and drying them for the winter.

All day long, the old lady patiently picked strawberries, wild raspberries, blackberries and bilberries, while her husband stored up hazelnuts, chestnuts and walnuts.

At the start of autumn the old lady made jams in her copper cauldron and filled the pots with the lovely red and black jelly.

'We will eat well this winter,' she said to her husband.

The old man cut down branches, sawed the big logs, and chopped the beech logs, which he stacked in the shed.

'What lovely fires we will have!' he said to his wife.

Winter came with its cold gusts of wind. The icy snow covered all the paths but the old couple were well prepared.

They sat cosily by the fire eating delicious home-grown food.

All their hard work seemed worth it. They could sit by the fire and know that their larder was full.

Suddenly they heard a knock at the door. A group of animals were standing out in the cold and looked hopefully at the old man as he opened the door. 'Come in, come in,' the old man offered.

'Come and warm yourselves with us,' the old lady added.

The hedgehog came in first, followed by the squirrels, the fox and the rabbits.

The birds perched on the branches of firewood and sang.

The owl settled on the mantelpiece.

How cosy they were, all together, and how gay the cottage in Pretty Wood was now, with such a large family.

The fire crackled with joy in the hearth.

But one day when the old couple had spent a long time outside bringing in wood, the old man and the old lady both caught a nasty chill.

Soon they had a fever.

'Out of the question to get out of bed,' said the fox. 'We are going to look after you.'

The rabbits prepared a potion of verbena and rosemary.

The fox and the hedgehog saved up logs and watched the fire.

The owl and all the birds of the wood settled on the bed to make a warm blanket of soft feathers. A blanket of friendship. A blanket that sang.

The day arrived when the old man and his wife felt well enough to get up. Once again they sat in front of the fire, telling stories and listening to what the animals of the forest had to say. And so it was that they passed the long winter evenings.

One fine morning they awoke to see buds of yellow down on the branches of the willow trees. The sun peeped through the branches. Spring had arrived.

The birds started to build their nests. They sang happily on the branches of the birch trees and soared into the sky.

It was good to be alive.

Baby Tiger Escapes

The baby tiger crouched between his mother's paws, looking as though butter wouldn't melt in his mouth. He looked up at her, his angelic face full of tender confidence.

What a joy the youngster was to Kitty, his mother. He had the most beautiful stripes and the most cheerful nature!

Mr and Mrs Dobson, owners of the two wild animals, had lived for a long time in southern Asia. Mrs Dobson had found Kitty there, wandering all alone. She adopted the animal and fed her from a bottle.

When it was time to return home, Kitty was expecting her first cub, and Mrs Dobson could not bear to leave the gentle tigress behind.

Her husband agreed. After all their grounds were large enough for Kitty to be able to play in peace, and they could have high walls built to stop an escape. In any case Kitty was so tame she would run up like a dog whenever her mistress called, so the dangers of escape could be ruled out.

Kitty adapted immediately to her new life. She enjoyed roaming by the stream and watching the first

steps of her son Jimmy, born soon after they settled in England.

There was so much happiness in the big white house! But in the village, tongues were wagging. There was far too much talk about 'man-eating' tigers living on the estate. When the postman delivered the mail, he shook every time he saw the shadows of the wild beasts silhouetted between the trees! One morning Mrs Dobson found Kitty scratching at the front door and moaning. Jimmy was nowhere to be seen.

Within minutes the whole house had been turned upside down. Jimmy had disappeared without trace.

The locals somehow found out about the missing cub and got together to talk. They set up a plan of attack. Carrying pitchforks and with grim looks on their faces, they set out to hunt the animal.

When they reached the grounds of the house, they did not hesitate to howl: 'Kill the tiger, kill him!'

Poor Kitty was terrified and trembled violently. Mrs Dobson stroked her head and tried to pacify her.

Poor Kitty who wouldn't harm a fly! And as for the cub, Jimmy, he had only just started to walk!

The excited locals cried, 'Give us the tiger! We'll burn your house down if we don't get him!'

Mrs Dobson put her face in her hands and started to cry. Mr Dobson felt his temper rising. He tried talking to the locals, who would not listen to him at first. Then Mr Dobson chose a different course. He listed, one by one, all the favours that he and his family had granted to the villagers, and spoke of those that he and his wife would continue

to grant, if they were left in peace.

The villagers bent their heads together and talked about it. They finally agreed to a compromise. 'We will give you till tonight to find your animal. After that we will hunt and kill it. We don't want a man-eating tiger attacking our wives and children . . .'

'The tigers are absolutely harmless,' cried Mrs Dobson, joining in the conversation for the first time. 'Kitty eats out of my hand and the one that's missing is only a cub.'

The villagers went back to their houses but the Dobsons went on searching far into the night. They knew how serious things could be if the cub was not found. They searched everywhere, sometimes calling, sometimes listening.

In the middle of the night they heard a strange cry. They rushed towards the sound and found Jimmy stuck at the top of a tall tree. Mr Dobson rescued him and gave him to Kitty. Poor Jimmy. He was so hungry and pleased to be back with his mother.

Tired but happy, they all went to bed.

The Bluebird's Birthday

It was the bluebird's birthday, and all the birds had decided to give him very unusual presents.

The weaver-birds wove a gorgeous carpet of straw and moss. The larks baked a pie with corn and the golden honey of the bees. The finches and the blackbirds decorated the bluebird's house. The magpie knitted a smart pullover. Every bird had found the ideal gift, except the tits. They had no imagination at all.

'They day will soon be over . . . oh, what can we do?' they lamented.

Just then a storm broke.

When it was over, a rainbow spread its halo over the woods.

'Let's take a little bit of its material,' suggested one adorable tit. 'We can soon sew a cloak for the handsome bluebird.'

The birds flew up quickly to the majestic rainbow which immediately gave them a piece of its lovely material, which they made into a beautiful cloak.

The bluebird could not believe his good fortune. He looked extremely handsome dressed in his birthday clothes. What a party they had! What singing! What dancing!

Oliver's Horse

'Quick, hurry up, chestnut horse! It's your turn to race. I have already put on my handsome green jockey's outfit. Get a move on, please,' implored Oliver.

The chestnut horse refused to budge an inch.

'But,' answered the chestnut horse, 'it's impossible!'

'Why?' asked Oliver.

'I've lost my blinkers!'

'I know what we'll do,' cried the grey donkey. 'Get on my back, Oliver, and we will go and find them quickly.'

Oliver jumped immediately on to the grey donkey's back. They would have to hurry if they were going to be able to take part in the race.

The donkey ran through the meadow. 'Hee Haw! Hee Haw!' he shouted as he went into the shed.

'Why are you shouting like that?' asked the cow. 'You'll wake up my calf who is sleeping.'

'Where are the blinkers of the chestnut horse?' asked Oliver.

The cow looked in the fresh straw of the shed and in the dark corners.

'Not here!' she said. 'No blinkers in the shed. Go and look somewhere else.'

Oliver jumped up on to the donkey again, and off they went.

The donkey ran through the meadow. 'Hee Haw! Hee Haw!'

'Why are you shouting like that?' asked the horse. 'You will wake up the young foals who are having a rest!'

'Where are the blinkers of the chestnut horse?' asked Oliver.

The horse looked in his trough and under the cobwebs.

'Not here!' he said. 'No blinkers in the stable. Go and look somewhere else!'

Off they trotted again. Oliver looked from right to left in case he should see the blinkers lying on the ground.

The donkey ran to the pigsty. 'Hee Haw!'

'Why are you shouting like that?' snorted the pink pig. 'You'll wake up my piglets who are having a rest!'

'Where are the blinkers of the chestnut horse?' asked Oliver.

The pig looked under the sleeping piglets.

'Not here,' she said. 'No blinkers here.'

The donkey ran to the hen-coop. 'Hee Haw! Hee Haw! Hee Haw!'

'Why are you shouting like that?'

asked the hens. 'You will wake up our sleeping chicks.'

'Where are the blinkers of the chestnut horse?'

The hens looked in the nests and pushed aside the eggs and the sleeping chicks.

'Not here,' they said. 'No blinkers in the hen-coop.'

The donkey ran to the rabbit hutch. 'Hee Haw! Hee Haw!'

'Why are you shouting so loud?' asked the rabbits. 'You will wake up our babies who are asleep.'

'Where are the blinkers of the chestnut horse?' asked Oliver.

The rabbits lifted up their bedding and looked under the pink clover and the big cabbage leaves.

'Not here,' they said. 'No blinkers in the hutch.'

The donkey ran towards the pond. 'Hee Haw! Hee Haw!'

'Why are you shouting so loud?' cried the ducks. 'You will frighten our ducklings who are having their swimming lesson!'

'Where are the blinkers of the chestnut horse?' asked Oliver.

The ducks looked in the reeds and sifted through the mud.

'Not here,' they said. 'No blinkers here.'

Oliver and the donkey felt very disheartened. It seemed as if they would never find the blinkers and Oliver would not be able to race on his beautiful chestnut horse.

Suddenly the green frog who was sleeping on a water-lily leaf opened her golden eyes.

Plop! She dived to the bottom of the water.

At last she came back up and said, 'Here are the blinkers belonging to the chestnut horse!'

The donkey ran to the race course immediately. 'Hee Haw! Hee Haw!'

'Here are your blinkers!' cried Oliver, happily.

The chestnut horse was very pleased.

Oliver, in his green jockey suit, jumped on to the back of the chestnut horse and they rode to the starting gate.

The other horses were having a practice gallop to stretch their legs.

Oliver and his horse also galloped about a bit, and Oliver could tell that he was in fine form.

'Get ready, jockeys. On your marks!'

But the young horses were frolicking left and right. They were in no hurry. It was good to play in the wind!

'Come along, my little chestnut horse,' said Oliver, stroking him. 'It's time to get in line.'

'Ready . . . steady . . . go!'

The chestnut horse was the last to go. But how he ran.

He caught up first with one horse, then another and yet another!

The finishing post was in sight as the chestnut horse strained to overtake the only horse in front of him. He wasn't quite fast enough, and came in second.

'Well done, chestnut horse!' cried Oliver, giving him a kiss. 'You ran really well. We didn't win but that doesn't matter. You galloped hard and we had a lot of fun.

'Thank you, friends, thank you,' cried the chestnut horse to all his friends who had been watching and cheering him on.

That is how the chestnut horse found his blinkers and raced well with his friend Oliver, the jockey in the green outfit.

The Cat and the Mouse

Miranda the mouse and Charlotte the grey cat had become inseparable friends. Charlotte's mistress was called Lily, and the cat loved her very much and spent a long time on her lap being stroked. This didn't go down very well with Barnaby the dog.

Barnaby was not a bad dog but he occasionally got jealous and took revenge by chasing the cat and eating her food.

When Barnaby saw the cat and mouse together for the first time, he gave them a hair-raising chase. The cat and mouse went to hide in the grocer's storeroom.

It was there that the cat and mouse met Thomas, the lazy tomcat belonging to the grocer. He had been locked in the storeroom to catch mice. 'You've nothing to worry about,' Charlotte assured Miranda. 'He's too lazy to catch you and he's sure to go out.'

'You do know a lot!' said Miranda. 'And look! Lily is taking Barnaby for a walk.'

'Time for fun,' said Charlotte winking. 'I'll mew lovingly. The tom will come out and Barnaby will do the rest.'

Indeed, Thomas, flattered by his pretty neighbour's visit, rounded his back and purred.

107

Barnaby had seen it all. He growled, the tom panicked and ran, chased by the dog.

The cat and mouse slipped in through the cat door.

Miranda was puzzled by a lump of cheese. 'Charlotte? Who can live in all the little rooms of that big house?'

'Nobody, silly. It's a round Gruyère cheese!'

'Cheese! What a feast!' and the little mouse nibbled her way right into the cheese and disappeared.

'You must come out, Miranda, it's time to go!' called Charlotte.

'I can't! I'm up against a wall on one side, and the holes have got smaller on the other!'

'The holes haven't got smaller, it's your tummy that's got bigger! Sshh . . . I smell Thomas.'

In Thomas walked. He was dirty, dishevelled, and had one eye scratched! 'That dog's crazy!' he mumbled. 'Do me a favour, Charlotte. Stay and keep watch. If my master were to find a hint of mouse droppings in his cheese he would give me such a hiding!'

'Don't worry, Thomas. I'll look after things here,' said Charlotte.

Charlotte waited for the tom to fall asleep and then called Miranda.

With Charlotte's help, Miranda got out of the cheese and the two friends beat a hasty retreat from that storeroom.

'Let's take a look at Barnaby,' suggested Miranda. 'I think he's in his kennel.'

'Hello, Barnaby,' said Charlotte as though nothing had happened. 'Well I never! Have you been in a fight?'

Eyes narrowed, and ears flat with rage, Barnaby growled, 'Cats and mice will be the death of me.'

'It's high time we all became friends,' said Charlotte. 'After all, Lily loves you as much as me.'

'All right,' Barnaby agreed at last. 'But don't expect me to like that cat next door.'

A Present From Heaven

The mouse children were playing on the swings. Minnie, the bravest, shouted at her sisters, 'Push! push! higher!'

They pushed so hard that the mouse flew off into the air and landed on the back of a passing stork.

'Why, a present from heaven!' exclaimed the stork, not in the least surprised. And she continued her journey towards a far-off country.

The stork's mission was to take new-born babies to certain homes in the East.

The stork journeyed on and on, but Minnie did not mind. In fact, she was thrilled by the adventure. She missed her family of course, but her dear parents had more than enough children to cope with.

The stork was reaching the end of her journey. She was drawn towards a little low house, surrounded by large flowering trees.

Landing on the balcony, she listened through the half-open window.

'Well, my dear wife, I think we must give up the hope of ever having a child of our own,' a mouse wearing trousers and smoking a pipe said.

Opposite him, his companion nodded in agreement. 'It's such a pity. There will be no one to leave our lovely house to, no one to pamper! How I would have loved being a mother.'

The stork did not hesitate. She flew to the chimney and slipped Minnie expertly down the dark tunnel.

Minnie landed with a light bump at the feet of Mr and Mrs Mouse.

How delighted they all were. Minnie had new parents and Mr and Mrs Mouse had a child of their own at last.

The Owl's Birthday

Susannah was happy for it was time to take her pet rabbit Lettuce for a walk in the forest.

Susannah picked a perfumed bouquet and sniffed it appreciatively.

'That smells good!' said Lettuce.

Susannah thought so too and soon filled her arms with flowers.

'Mummy will be very pleased,' she said.

A cuckoo landed on Susannah's shoulder. 'Shall we play hide-and-seek?'

Susannah and Lettuce agreed eagerly.

After the game of hide-and-seek, Susannah danced and skipped and sang until quite suddenly it was

nightfall and time to go home.

Sadly they tried to find the path home. But every path looked the same in the gathering gloom.

Luckily, the owls came to their rescue and showed them the way through the forest lit by fireflies, and into a large clearing bathed in the bluish light of the moon.

All of a sudden sounds of shrieks of happy laughter rang in the place which was filled with all sorts of animals!

'What is going on?' Susannah asked Lettuce, astounded.

'I would very much like to know,' replied Lettuce, as baffled as she was.

'It's Hullabaloo's birthday,' hooted the owls in chorus.

Hullabaloo was a large brown owl and he stood resplendent, conducting the blackbird orchestra with a switch of hazel. The rabbits whirled with the foxes and the weasels asked the wild geese to dance.

Susannah could not resist, and joined in the fun. She stood in the middle of the animals dancing first with Lettuce, then with each fox. Flushed with excitement, Susannah was dishevelled and out of breath, but she did not care: she was having so much fun!

'Sing with us,' whistled the blackbirds.

Susannah did not need to be asked twice and she made up a song.

'Bravo, bravo!' applauded all the animals when she had finished.

'Now we must refresh ourselves to restore our spirits,' said Hullabaloo as he gallantly offered his right wing to Susannah.

Everyone drank Hullabaloo's special nectar and ate wild honey. It was a delicious combination and the little girl had quite a feast.

Then just as suddenly as it had come, the night was gone. In its place was the pink dawn, which disbanded the guests, happy but weary after such a night.

Susannah and Lettuce slipped quietly back home. Susannah popped quickly into bed, where she closed her eyes on her lovely memory. No one had noticed her absence and that is just as well, for Susannah had no intention of telling anyone about her wonderful adventure.

A Story All in White

A young lamb, a little ball of snowy white, was gambolling in the green meadow. His mother, the kindly ewe, watched him lovingly.

He chased the butterflies and tried to catch the birds. He blew on the water of the stream and poked the tip of his pink nose into the petals of the summer flowers.

His big eyes sparkled with mischief; innocently open wide, they had an impish look.

Sometimes he dreamed of open spaces and freedom. Then he would go to the hawthorn hedge which separated him from the enormous forest, and look out. It seemed to him to be a place of secrets and magic, closed to him. His parents would not allow him to venture far.

What went on under those big green trees? What mystery were they hiding from him? Through the hole in the hedge, he sniffed the scented air from that fascinating mass of greenery.

'Snowball, come here! You know that I have forbidden you to go near the hedge!' said his mother.

So, hanging his head with disappointment, Snowball would come back to her side with a sigh. The big adventure would have to wait for another day!

Autumn powdered the big trees of the forest with gold dust. And the lamb, a little bigger now, gazed at this enchantment, lamenting, 'Oh,

if only Mother would let me . . . I would go right over there, feast my eyes on wonders unknown, feast my heart on freedom.' Yes, but Mother had forbidden it.

Each morning he tried to summon up the necessary courage to defy her, but he never felt quite brave enough.

One morning, while his mother was eating breakfast, he slipped through the hawthorn hedge. He ran as fast as he could towards the glittering trees. He ran so fast that his hooves hardly touched the ground.

So it was that Snowball joined in the wild dancing of the plump mushrooms; that he rolled on the moss with the shiny chestnuts; that he waltzed with the glistening leaves that fell from the trees, plucked by the autumn wind.

Dizzy and breathless, he threw himself down next to a tree stump.

He needed to collect his thoughts. His friends ran away laughing, leaving him quite alone.

All at once, he felt cold and hungry. He was terribly weary. Being free was no fun at all any more. What he needed was his mother. He longed to nestle close by her side. He wanted to bury his face in her warm fleece.

He had to find the way back to his green meadow. But in this tangle of bushes and undergrowth, how was he to get out?

He had danced and pranced around for so long that he had quite lost himself. He was deep in the forest and all the trees looked the same to him.

'Baa, baa! Mother, where are you? Come and fetch me!'

Alas, only the echo answered his cries . . . baa . . . baa . . .

He sniffed and just then a genie wearing big brown boots appeared before him. He had sprung from

somewhere in the thicket and now he blocked the way with a menacing look.

'So, little intruder, you want to interrupt our merrymaking?'

'But sir, your forest is so beautiful that I couldn't help it.'

'I see! To punish you, I am going to turn you into a cloud,' said the genie, blowing on Snowball.

And the lamb was sent to graze in the blue sky.

He was very unhappy and lonely, perched right up there. He could see his pretty mother, so far away, and he called her. But she could not hear him. His voice was like the wind sighing, and she did not notice it.

So the little lamb cloud started to cry. He cried so hard and so long that in the morning a thick layer of snow covered the earth.

Because of so much crying, the cloud shrank and became so small that . . . suddenly the lamb woke up

from his awful nightmare. He was nice and warm, and cuddled up to his mother in the sheep pen.

He sighed. Then, with his big eyes heavy with sleep, he murmured, yawning, 'a cloud in the sky . . a snowflake on the earth.'

He much preferred being just a little lamb.

Smiling at his mother, Snowball fell asleep again, comforted. Next spring, he would see his green meadow again. How pretty it would be, all strewn with daisies and glittering with buttercups. He would gambol there, drunk with happiness and freedom. He had no more desire to venture into the big, strange forest.

Outside, the snow fell in big flakes, while in the scented straw a lamb dreamed of spring blossoms.

Playing Truant

Flip Squirrel hated school, especially when the sun was shining. That day the fine weather invited him to walk in the nearby woods. Good-bye school! The naughty squirrel went off to look for hazelnuts.

Flip ventured near a pond covered with pink water-lilies. He decided to pick some and jumped into an old moss-covered boat. Alas! He very quickly found out that it leaked in a dozen places. Flip tried to get back to the bank and rowed as fast as he could. Too late; the boat sank and left Flip struggling in the water.

Finally, Flip managed to reach dry land again and decided that school was better than drowning. He hurried along and took a short cut across a field.

A gander whose field it was, was not too pleased about the intruder and chased Flip up a tree. He had to wait a long time for the gander to go away before he could come down.

Flip never played truant again.

The Silly Goose

Settled on her soft straw nest, Agatha, the finest goose on the farm, was hatching six lovely eggs. It would be quite an event. Her first brood, since Agatha proudly wore round her snowy neck the wide red sash which denoted first prize at the agricultural fair.

When the little geese were born they waddled obediently behind their mother. Alas! Agatha had to reprimand the smallest and the naughtiest of her daughters, little Zara, all the time. Ten times she had got lost under the lettuces in the vegetable garden. Once she got stuck under the thorny hedges. She had cried very loudly, and called her mother to the rescue in her noisy tearful voice. But she seemed to have learned nothing from this lesson at all, and was still as naughty and unreliable as ever.

The geese grew up a bit more and, like all good girls, had to go to school. Only one strayed from the path, and that was Zara. The rascal skipped about, splashing her sisters by jumping in the puddles. Their new school aprons and exercise books got stained.

Tom, Zara's favourite playmate, was always encouraging her to be naughty. Tom was a real scoundrel, and looked like one, with his cheeky nose and brown ring round one eye. Zara would perch on his back, and the naughty pair would ring door-bells or wave the big white sheets drying in the gardens.

'Hoo, hoo,' Tom would moan, as Zara waggled the sheets at the kittens in a most frightening way.

'Mummy! Mummy! A ghost!' the terrified kittens would miaouw and race indoors.

Mrs Owl, the teacher, pointed to the letters on the blackboard. The whole class was concentrating. The rabbit wrinkled his nose and moved his long ears. The red hen beat her wings and clucked studiously. All the animals copied the letters industriously into their exercise books. All, that is, except for Zara, who felt there were other, more exciting things to do.

In the room, hidden behind the

raised lid of her desk, Zara was dreamily plaiting a crown of daisies. Mrs Owl told her off and sent her to stand in the corner wearing the dunce's hat. But as naughty as ever, the next day Zara played truant to go and see the circus. Tom had seen the big top go up in the village square. So the two villains had hidden under a bench to watch the rehearsals.

They heard the circus master lamenting that the performing donkey was ill.

'I will take his place,' offered Zara.

Mr Lloyd was delighted and hired her for that very evening. Zara, flushed with pride, ran to put on her best frilly dress and matching bonnet.

The whole village was there that evening. Mrs Owl together with all her pupils sat in the front row of the audience. The clowns were a great success. The dancers and the trapeze artistes too, received much applause, but now at last it was Zara's turn. Mr Lloyd entered the ring followed by Zara and they were greeted by long cheers.

'There's our Zara! Bravo! Bravo!' shouted the audience, who all knew Zara well, and were delighted to see her.

'Miss Zara,' thundered Mr Lloyd in his deep voice. 'Miss Zara, show us how intelligent you are. Tell me the sum of two and three.'

'Er . . . four, or it might well be six,' mumbled Zara stupidly.

The audience quivered with joy. Mrs Owl shut her big golden eyes in dismay and ruffled her feathers to show her indignation.

Mr Lloyd was white with fury and shook with rage. 'Four or six, you silly goose!' he shouted angrily. 'It makes five, stupid fool. Get out! You've ruined me!'

Zara ran away crying with shame, followed by the shouts of the crowd chanting 'Silly goose! Silly goose!' She took refuge with her mother.

Mother Goose loved her scatter-brained daughter very much and set about consoling her. Afterwards she gave her a lecture. 'My child, you see how stupid you made yourself look in front of all those people? Perhaps now you will listen to Mrs Owl's lessons and try harder.'

Hugged up close against the soft white feathers, Zara promised to do her best at school.

The next morning, the teacher found at her door a tearful young goose whose big tears soaked her doormat.

'Oh please, I don't want to be called a "silly goose" any more, Mrs Owl. Please teach me to add up and to read.'

'Hmmm,' grumbled the kind owl softly, 'let's hope that your good intentions will last through the months to come. Anyway, I'm willing to try, so what are we waiting for? To work little one! We've got to catch up on a lot of lessons. You will have to give up your playtime too.'

A little heavy-hearted, Zara gave her word and said good-bye to Tom, her companion on so many escapades in the nearby undergrowth. And from then on, there was no better behaved or more attentive pupil than Zara.

At the end of the year, Zara left the class proudly, her white feathers crowned with a laurel wreath. She carried under her wings prizes of books with gold-edged pages.

Good sport that he was, Tom was there to applaud her success, but he quickly ran off because he was scared that Mrs Owl would shut him in her classroom.

Tom would always be a 'silly goose'.

Mary's Clogs

It was Little Mary's birthday and she was overjoyed to receive as a present a pair of wooden clogs.

Mary was so pretty and so sweet that everybody loved her. They were all so pleased her birthday wish had come true. One young puppy called Tinker let his excitement get the better of him, and he had an irresistible urge to carry off one of the clogs. Tinker ran towards the river with the clog in his mouth when . . . splash . . . he had dropped it in the water and then fell in himself.

Mary helped Tinker out of the water and for the first time the naughty puppy saw her red eyes. He realised how silly he had been and ran along the bank following the clog, which was drifting away.

A kingfisher spotted the shoe and landed on it, wings outstretched. How pretty it was! A water rat wandering past rubbed his dazzled eyes!

Under the bridge, a low-hanging branch stopped the clog from continuing its journey and the kingfisher flew away.

Despite his fear of the fast-running water, the dog jumped in and seized the clog, which he brought back to Mary. She was so happy that she clasped both the clog and the puppy in her arms. They were still friends.

Journey to the Land of Roses

One fine summer's day, Lilian the ladybird went to see her friend the grasshopper. 'The Queen of the Roses is getting married and has invited us to the grand ball she is giving to celebrate! Come along, we ought to start our journey now,' she told him with great excitement.

The grasshopper, who was a musician, just had time to grab his violin and follow the ladybird.

They both walked for a long time along the path which led to the Land of Roses. Worn out with tiredness they soon had to stop. They felt far too hot to go on. It seemed to them that it might be better to cool down where they were, and then return home.

Then Lilian had a bright idea. 'Let's make a carriage out of a nutshell,' she said. 'But, oh dear! We

don't have anyone to pull it!'

Miss Caterpillar, busy nibbling a leaf at the time, pricked up her ears and suggested, shyly, 'If you like, I will pull the nutshell!'

The ladybird and the grasshopper looked at her with delight. They consulted together for a while about whether the caterpillar would be strong enough. After some consideration her proposal was accepted enthusiastically and the two friends harnessed the caterpillar with a pretty ribbon. Now they were on their way! As it went along, the strange carriage met a brightly coloured butterfly who wanted to join them and, further on, two sparrows joined in too.

All the creatures were very happy and sang at the tops of their voices, accompanied by the grasshopper on the violin. At last they arrived in the Land of Roses!

The Queen of the Roses looked radiant in her dress of white as she stood next to her bridegroom. He was a simple cornflower who seemed very happy. The Queen was overcome as she greeted her guests, and tears of joy ran down her petals making her even more beautiful.

The ceremony took place amid great rejoicing and the ball began. They danced all night long. Never in the memory of the flowers had there been such a wonderful occasion in the Land of the Roses.

Clarence Looks For a Master

Clarence was downhearted.

He was going to the market to be sold. In the van which was taking him to the market town, Clarence reflected on his young life. He was a handsome calf and that is why the farmer had picked him out to be sold.

'And yet,' he moaned, 'I had everything to make me happy! Good food . . . a nice straw bed and a big field in which to prance around.'

Clarence cried.

Suddenly the van stopped. It was the end of the journey for Clarence.

The young calf was tied to a fence next to an enormous bull. 'My name is Hercules the bull!' he bellowed into Clarence's ear, and the calf jumped with fright.

A farmer was deciding whether to buy Clarence, but eventually decided that the calf looked unfriendly.

Clarence was very worried by it all. Then he felt a gentle hand sliding along his neck and he lifted up his head.

'You look ever so unhappy!' a little boy said to him.

Instinctively, the calf knew that the boy looking at him was a friend.

Clarence nestled up to the child who said to him softly, 'Would you like to live with me?'

The child went running off and Clarence didn't know where he had gone. Then a farmer, who was interested in Clarence, bought him without further ado.

The calf was desperate, and pulled on his halter to escape. Suddenly he heard a shout, 'Hey! That calf belongs to me!'

'Too late!' replied both the seller and the buyer.

But the young man would not take no for an answer. He and Clarence were firm friends, he explained to them both.

Stubbornly the boy stood his ground until finally the farmer relented.

Clarence was happy again. Everything had turned out for the best. 'We're going to get on well!' the boy whispered into his new friend's ear.

The young calf followed his new

master gladly. In no time at all there was a perfect understanding between them. He followed him through the crowd, head high, eyes shining. He was so docile that more than one passer-by was surprised.

Clarence was growing up. He loved the freedom of his new home on a farm in the middle of the country. His stall was comfortable, and the field grass that he ate all day long was as sweet as the dew.

As Clarence became more and more attached to his young master, he followed him everywhere, which made the boy happy too. And every day, Clarence accompanied him to and from school at his slow and easy pace. In the village, it was quite an event to behold. His reputation as a tame bull calf aroused the admiration of all.

As far as the boy was concerned, Clarence was no ordinary calf but a real companion. Clarence let himself be harnessed to the cart which his master drove. But if anyone else tried to harness him, he lashed out with his hooves.

Clarence the calf was as happy as he could be.

Soon the calf would be big enough to work in the fields with the boy. Clarence couldn't wait to grow up.

Trip and the Piglets

Once upon a time there was a young wild boar called Trip who was very sweet-looking. He had rounded flanks striped in brown and his slender legs were shoed with shiny hooves.

All day Trip trotted in the forest with his five brothers and sisters and his mother. Mother Boar turned the soil with her strong snout to uncover acorns and roots.

Trip was by nature kind and sociable, and as soon as he saw a hare or a badger he would run up to them grunting with pleasure.

But oh dear! At the sight of Mother Boar's massive shadow Trip's playmates would all run away. They knew of her bad temper. Poor Trip would be left quite crestfallen.

One day though, as he raced after a rabbit, Trip left the familiar trees far behind him. He came out into a clearing where there stood a tiny house. Trotting curiously round the fenced garden, the astonished boar stopped in front of a sandy area where a family of fat pink piglets was frolicking. Some new friends! For a while Trip and the little piglets played together. Mother Boar was not there to frighten them away. Soon they were all feeling hungry. An appetising gruel was steaming in a stone trough. The sight of it made Trip's mouth water. Grunting with impatience, he stood up on his back legs.

'Mummy!' one of the little pigs called 'We've got a visitor!'

At that precise moment the rusty fence gave way and Trip, taken by surprise, tumbled into the pen between Mother Sow's feet.

In astonishment she helped him up gently with her head. 'But it's a boar! Our cousin from the forest. What are you doing here?'

A little giddy, Trip sat down and started to recount his misadventure. 'I was a bit fed up in my forest where nobody wanted to play with me. So I chased a little wild rabbit. And now I think I'm really lost and I'm so hungry . . .'

'Children, make room for your

cousin,' Mother Sow ordered.

Mmm! The mash of rye mixed with potatoes was delicious! Trip had never eaten anything so good. Afterwards, feeling quite himself again, he played with the little pigs once more. Chasing each other and squeaking in high-pitched voices, they were making a fine row. But already the sun was going down on the horizon.

'You had better leave now, little one,' advised Mother Sow. 'The farmer will soon be back and he will make short work of catching you. Follow the line of chestnut trees along the edge of the forest and take the path planted with big oak trees. It's on the boars' route, as they find their favourite food there. I am sure your mother will be nearby looking for you!'

A little sadly, Trip took leave of his new friends and, slipping through the gap in the fence, reached the cover of the forest as fast as his legs would carry him.

Soon he caught sight of Mother Boar's dark shape as she anxiously scoured the undergrowth looking for him. Then, together, the whole family made its way home.

Trip, a little tired, lagged behind. But he promised himself that he would go back often to play with his cousins on the farm.

'Be very careful, young hothead,' his mother said. 'Men are very fond of the taste of boar. The farmer would get a good price for you at the hunters' lodge.'

Then Trip remembered the similar warning that the kind Mother Sow had given him. He swore to himself to be very careful and not to go near the house in the woods until nightfall—when the farmer with the fearful appetite would be tucked up in bed.

The Lost Cub

All was calm . . . The seagulls and cormorants drifted silently in the clear sky. The penguins strolled quietly about. Their wings were spread to make the most of the smallest ray of the comforting warmth of the Arctic summer sun. A little further on, white bears and seals were resting on the pebble beach. They had flopped down with their rounded stomachs towards the brilliant sun. How serene it was.

Everyone was quietly enjoying themselves in whichever way they liked best. There were no fights or quarrels. They were all friends.

Mother Bear decided to take a dip in the sea as a shoal of haddock was passing, for she was very hungry! 'Sylvester, come here!' she called to her friend the penguin. 'Will you keep an eye on my son Timothy while I am gone? Be especially watchful for he's a little rascal!' Mother Bear never knew what Timothy would do next, he was so mischievous.

But the bear cub was sleeping and his baby-sitter merely had to glance at him from time to time. Reassured by his stillness, Sylvester left his post and joined a group of Eskimo hunters who had just landed in their hide-covered kayaks. Sylvester saw among them his friend Yakohoua, who gave him a big wave. He was happy to see his wide smile again, which lifted his shiny, apricot-coloured cheeks.

129

Sylvester liked the black almond-shaped eyes and the frank laughing face of Yakohoua, who was a great hunter but never killed for the sake of it. The hardships of the Arctic winter oblige the Eskimos to eat seal meat and fat, but Yakohoua hunted only for what he needed and never for trading purposes.

The penguin had noticed this restraint in Sylvester, and admired him for it. It made him feel he could trust the man.

The two friends exchanged tidings on the ice-bank and Sylvester quite forgot his charge. Time passed quickly, and when Yakohoua rejoined the members of his tribe, Sylvester saw to his horror that Timothy had disappeared. He was dumbfounded, and his cries of panic woke up the sleepers. 'Timothy isn't here any more! Timothy's gone! What will Mother Bear say! Help me! Help me

to find him before she comes back!'

Everyone took part in the search, eyes half-closed, still sleepy. 'Timothy! Timothy!' they cried.

The penguins spread out in all directions, flapping their wings and calling to the runaway. There were thousands of them scouring the length and breadth of the ice-bank. Their black and white uniforms standing out against the spotless ice.

The bears joined the search party too and lumbered along to help their friends. Even the seals, with their enormous bulk, aroused themselves from their lethargy to crawl in the wake of the bears, who were hardly any faster than themselves. Everyone was concerned. They liked Sylvester and weren't happy to see him troubled. They also liked little Timothy with his merry ways, and wanted to find him quickly. They knew his mother would be terribly upset when she returned to find him gone.

The birds scoured the beach and the sky quivered with the beating of their wings. Not one of the ice-bank's inhabitants was idle, and there was much commotion in that once serene place.

The day was over for the Eskimos. Their kayaks were brimming over

with seal meat that would soon be drying in the sun. These were their provisions for the long winter which would soon be upon them and the oarsmen rowed carefully so as not to capsize their precious cargo. Yakohoua passed the beach and took the opportunity to wave good-bye: 'Hey! What's going on?' Yakohoua shouted to his companions.

'We haven't the foggiest idea. They all seem to have gone a bit mad, rushing about and trying to shout louder than each other!'

But Yakohoua couldn't accept that explanation. He knew his animal friends better than that.

'Let's go and see. Perhaps we can help . . .'

The Eskimos disembarked on the beach and had great difficulty in getting someone to explain the situation to them.

'Mother Bear left her cub in Sylvester's charge, and that scatter-brain left him on his own and now he's lost . . .' a breathless penguin told them over his shoulder as he rushed past.

The hunters joined in with the madness. Soon their lovely colourful suits mingled with the dark tones of the seals and penguins. Time went

quickly by and finally everybody was exhausted.

Little by little, calm returned. Everyone had a rest, catching his breath and collecting his spirits. 'Mother Bear is too far away to see what is happening here. Just as well . . . she's not exactly easy-going, even with those that she likes!' the animals agreed amongst themselves. Even the hunters were nervous of Mother Bear, and knew her wrath could be terrible if she felt her children had come to harm.

Sylvester was shaking with sobs and nothing could comfort him. 'I am dishonoured . . . I'm lost . . .' and he threw himself on to a pile of snow.

Crash! The pile of snow was warm. It moved, it shook itself, and the weeping penguin was sent flying, nose down in the frozen snow. 'What's happening to me?' cried the miserable penguin.

'What are you doing there, Sylvester?' asked a small bear-like voice.

The pile of snow? It was the bear cub quietly taking a nap, like everyone else.

'I was cold and rolled myself into a ball with my nose in my thick fur. What did you have to wake me up for, using my back as an armchair? What funny manners.'

Sylvester switched from despair to anger. 'Fancy hiding! Fancy camouflaging yourself in the snow, while we were looking for you everywhere! All the time you were sleeping peacefully, deaf to our calls. What selfishness!'

Mother Bear arrived just in time to break up the quarrel. She listened to the story of this adventure and soothed the ruffled tempers. 'Sylvester, when someone asks you a favour and you accept, then you must fulfil it very conscientiously, and put off until later your games and fun. As for you, my son, you are a bit too mischievous and I am not sure that this wasn't your idea of a joke.'

And that was the end of the adventure that set the small population of the ice-bank into frenzied activity one fine afternoon in the Arctic summer. Everyone scattered without further ado to finish their much-needed naps.

132

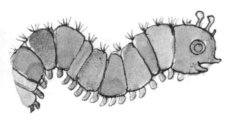

A Day in Spring

One, two, three, ten, twenty pairs of green feet clung to the thickest branch of a purple flower. It was Delia, the ugly green caterpillar. She was so enormous, fat and shiny, that despite her bright green colour, no one dared come near her. Sad and lonely, she gave in to the sleepiness that was irresistibly coming over her. She only had time to throw out a few threads to weave her cocoon before she fell asleep, exhausted. After several days the few friends she did have were getting worried. Surely she must be dead? But no! It's spring and life is reborn!

Delia woke up, broke her cocoon, and after hours of effort, regained her freedom. Finally, under the wondering gaze of her friends, she could admire the two huge wings, bursting with colour, that were fixed to her back. She opened them, closed them, amazed. She was no longer Delia, the ugly green caterpillar, but had become a beautiful butterfly!

The Rabbit and the Fox

Leo, the wild rabbit, went off to look for an adventure in a happy mood. He crossed the heath perfumed with lavender and marjoram, and came to a halt in front of a ball of fur asleep at the foot of an old tree. It looked like Master Fox! Leo was ready to bolt, but two enormous black eyes stared at him in astonishment and said, 'Hello! Who are you?'

'I . . . I . . . am Leo. And you?'

'My name is Fred, the desert fox.'

'Then you're not a real fox?'

'I know I look very much like that distant cousin of mine, but actually I've come from the Sahara. I'm so hungry and tired.'

'Come with me, I'll introduce you to my friends and we will go and visit Nannie,' suggested Leo.

'Who is Nannie?' asked the desert fox.

'She's a very kind grandmother. She will look after you.'

The new friends went off happily together.

'Oh! It's almost like my home-land,' exclaimed Fred. 'But the air is more fragrant. What are those strange sounds?'

'The grasshoppers and the crickets who sing all the time in summer.'

Soon the two friends arrived in front of Nannie's house, a white-washed cottage covered with flowers.

Nannie welcomed them warmly, since they would cheer her long lonely hours. Her tender look lingered on Fred as she admired his almond eyes, his huge ears and his soft honey-coloured fur.

'Come in and rest, my friends,' she said. 'You can tell me all about your adventures afterwards.'

Fred was grateful for the saucer of milk and, with his spirits restored, started his story. He told of his cap-

ture, the journey in the overheated hold of the ship, the accident with the lorry that was taking him to the zoo, his escape, his meeting with Leo . . .

'That's all very well,' said Nannie thoughtfully. 'You can live with Leo and his friends for the time being but what will you do when the winter comes?'

Fred was saddened; he was only thinking of his present happiness. He was still too young and carefree to worry about the hard times, or think of the future, and Leo was too scatter-brained to think of warning him.

'What will become of me?' cried Fred in a panic. 'I don't want to spend my life locked up in a zoo!'

'There's no question about it,' interrupted Nannie gently. 'You can keep me company and I will keep you warm during the cold season.'

Leo came to see them every morning and the three of them spent their days in peace and joy.

Why don't you go and say hello to Nannie, Leo and Fred? If you can find them.

The Snow Hare

Lionel the little snow hare was born on a spring day, with his four brothers, as the sun started to warm the green grass.

In her burrow of grass and leaves, Mother Hare stroked her leverets and gave them milk. Lionel nestled up to his mother's warm fur. He was a happy little hare.

'Come and see, little ones,' said Mother Hare. 'The sky has turned to blue over the white mountains.'

The young leverets jostled to get out of the burrow. How good it felt to stretch in the sunshine and frolic among the daisies! The world seemed so big to Lionel, the snow hare! Lionel breathed the crisp air of the mountain and sniffed the first spring flowers.

When summer came the hares played hide-and-seek under the rhododendrons and the blueberries, then rested in the shade of a pine tree.

But golden autumn brought frightening noises across the mountain.

'Bang! Bang! Bang! Bang!'
'Mummy, what is it?' asked Lionel.
'The hunters. Quick, run for the burrow!' called his mother urgently.

When winter covered the mountain with snow, and hid the green pines and the rocks, the leverets looked at themselves.

'Mummy,' cried Lionel, 'I don't recognize myself!'

'You have grown lovely white fur, Lionel,' said his mother. 'You will be like this every winter so that you can hide more easily in the snow if you are in danger.'

'I see!' answered Lionel. 'Well, I'm very pleased. I think I'm very handsome.'

Lionel liked to run on the snow, jump over the crevices and slide on

Lionel could feel his heart pounding in his chest. Desperately he jumped over one crevice, then another and threw himself against the cliff.

However the eagle with his piercing eyes had seen the little white hare and swooped suddenly down. But clever Lionel slipped inside a deep cleft in the rock and kept very still.

The little snow hare was saved.

What a fright he had had! And how happy he was to see, right at the end of the rock, a little white cloud floating in a patch of blue sky!

the ice. 'Hey, this is fun!' cried the little hare.

There was a girl coming down on skis. Crash! The girl was lying in the snow, her skis in the air.

Lionel laughed, safe under a pine tree and said, 'I slide on my paws, like this!'

And whoosh! Lionel sped down the slope.

One day, Lionel was doing pirouettes on the sparkling frozen snow when a big black shadow came down in the blue sky and moved nearer without a sound.

Lionel looked up and started to run.

The big shadow flew closer to the ground. 'Oh!' said Lionel as he looked up again. 'An eagle!'

Hop! Lionel jumped as hard as he could and turned suddenly. In the sky the eagle beat his great wings and whirled too.

Lionel saw the black shadow on the dazzling snow getting closer and closer.

Faster, faster, Lionel went!

The Persian and the Moggy

Charley was a cat, but not just any old cat, as he knew only too well. Charley was a fine Persian cat, and all the friends of Oliver, his master, liked him because he was very handsome.

But Charley was unbearable and thought that his pedigree entitled him to be bad-tempered.

'What! Midday and my lunch is not served. It's scandalous.'

Yet Oliver looked after his friend. He now gently placed in front of him a plate of food, heated to just the right temperature. 'I will eat it, if and when I like,' thought Charley.

He finally made up his mind and delicately ate from the proffered plate.

Having finished his meal, Charley, with a quiet measured tread, went back to the velvet armchair, which was his throne, and slowly licked his paws.

But suddenly, Charley couldn't believe his eyes. Right in front of him, outside the window, a half-starved alley cat was watching him with big yellow eyes. 'Well, I ask you!' thought Charley indignantly. 'What is that vulgar moggy doing in my garden?'

And he leaped up, his whiskers bristling, his fur standing on end, his eyes popping out of their sockets.

The poor stray cat ran away without asking for leftovers; he had found no sympathy with the lord of the manor.

All the same, next day he was back.

Charley chased off the intruder again and was proud of it, especially

as it happened several days running.

One fine afternoon with spring in the air, Charley decided to go for a walk near the molehill, to give the moles a fright.

In his haste, he had not noticed two suspicious looking individuals who were watching him with interest.

'It's a Blue Persian,' said one. 'They're worth a lot.'

'Let's seize him,' said the other delightedly, and his hand came down heavily on the delicate neck.

'Miaow,' cried Charley outraged, trying to struggle out of the grip. 'Where are your manners?'

Unfortunately for him, his escapade seemed bound to end badly. Until suddenly one of the men shouted with pain and dropped him.

Who could have come to his rescue like that?

His saviour was none other than the half-starved cat.

Seeing the Persian in danger, the alley cat had not hesitated to scratch and bite the man who had seized Charley.

'Miaow, I am very grateful,' said Charley, smiling at his new friend. 'You have quite simply saved my life. Would you like to come home with me?'

The alley cat could hardly believe his ears and purred with pleasure. 'Miaow, I'd be delighted,' he said, shaking Charley's paw.

As for the two men, they had already run away.

Meanwhile, Oliver was reading a book, lying on the living room carpet. He wondered where the Persian could have got to. He had called him several times in vain. 'I expect he is wandering about nearby,' he thought hopefully.

All of a sudden a miaowing disturbed his reading. Charley, with his new friend at his heels, came into the room.

'Who is that?' cried Oliver in amazement, seeing the unexpected visitor.

'He's my friend,' declared Charley, blushing a bit. 'He saved me from two men. 'He is very nice and very brave.'

'Well, well,' replied Oliver. 'You're very charming all of a sudden, Charley.' He looked at the alley cat and offered him a hearty meal, which delighted the poor starved creature.

'I think you were hungry,' said Oliver, taking the cat gently in his arms and stroking him. 'We'll keep you, if you like.'

'We shall always be friends,' Charley promised, purring.

'I am happy to see you behave this way,' remarked Oliver.

Charley took his place on the armchair that he now shared with the moggy called Tigger.

The two cats were bound by friendship from then on.

'Beauty is nothing, friendship is everything,' miaowed Charley.

Oliver and Tigger agreed with him wholeheartedly.

The Great Race

Paul slowed down his pace. A few more steps and then he collapsed in the shade of the nearest tree. His heart was beating fit to burst. Beads of perspiration covered his high brown forehead. He panted, trying to get air into his choked lungs.

Anoua, the leopard, came to join him, trotting nimbly, cool and fit. 'How fast you are!' gasped Paul, still out of breath.

'Obviously! You see my whole body is built for running! I have to catch the fastest prey and flee my enemies . . . Why do you persist in trying to match me? I will always win!' she boasted scornfully.

'Are you quite sure of that?' muttered Paul. 'I've got an idea for tomorrow. Meet me here, and we will have a race.'

Next day at dawn, when the air was still cool, Paul ran to see his friend Bob, the safari guide. He asked if he could ride in one of the Land Rovers . . .

With Bob's permission, Paul took up position on the back platform of the jeep, without even bothering to find out which way it was going.

Anoua, muscles flexed, ready for the off, was astounded to be overtaken by Paul, who clapped his hands and burst out laughing. Anoua resigned himself to the trick that his friend had played on him like a good sport. He pretended to put up a fight in a race that he knew was lost to him from the start. He could already imagine how exultant the winner would be and got ready to admit defeat.

But the jeep didn't stop and to Anoua's great surprise he saw it disappear in a cloud of dust. Paul shouted for the driver to stop, but he could not be heard over the roar of the engine. Many hours later, Paul returned. He was drenched with perspiration and bent double with exhaustion, and he found Anoua peacefully resting in the shade of a huge mango tree. 'What a race! And what a scare I got! But if it had worked, I would have won!'

'What a terror you are!' replied Anoua kindly. 'You must always have the last word, mustn't you? But I'll forgive you. What about another race tomorrow?'

143

The Cow and the Fox

A nice fat cow, well rounded and rusty coloured, was grazing grass.

A young fox happened to pass by. 'Hey, my good woman,' he said. 'Shall we cultivate a field between us? I will help you to plough, sow and reap and we could share the harvest half each. To avoid any arguments, I will take everything that grows above the ground and you can take everything that grows underneath.'

'All right,' replied the cow.

And they set about pulling the plough.

'Phew, it's so tiring!' said the fox. 'I will leave you to work alone, my friend.'

The cow privately thought that the fox wasn't very energetic, but nevertheless went on ploughing on her own. She also sowed and weeded.

The fox watched her work, dreaming of the harvest and the money. From time to time, he called to the cow. 'Chin up, my good woman! You're working well.'

When the time came for the harvest, the fox ran to fetch a big

cart. 'Let's share out the crop,' he said. 'Everything that has grown above the ground is mine, everything that has grown in the earth is yours!'

'Yes,' replied the cow. 'As it happens, I planted potatoes. You can take the leaves, I'm going to dig up the vegetables.'

So the fox watched the cow go off with the cart full of potatoes, and sat by a pile of useless leaves.

'Aha!' said the fox to himself. 'It looks as though that cow has made a fool of me! But just you wait.'

When the cow came back from the market with a basket full of big coins, the fox was waiting for her under the apple tree. 'Well my friend,' he said, 'I really enjoyed working with you. Let's do it again this year. But this time I will take everything that grows in the earth and you take everything that grows on top of it.'

'It's a deal,' the cow replied. And she started pulling the plough again, sowing, and harrowing, while the fox watched her work.

'Come along now, chin up!' he called to her, sucking at a daisy.

When harvest time came, the fox arrived with three big carts. 'You remember our agreement?' he said. 'Everything that's grown underneath is mine, but everything that's grown on top is yours.'

'Of course,' the cow replied. 'It so happens that this year I've planted corn. You can take the roots. I am keeping the ears.'

And the cow went off with the three big carts full of corn, while the fox quivered with rage in the middle of the empty field.

'That cow has made a fool of me twice,' growled the fox, 'but it won't happen again! I'm going to show her that foxes are the craftiest animals!'

When the cow came back from the market with her basket full of big coins, the fox was waiting for her under the apple tree.

'This time,' he told her very angrily and showing his teeth, 'I will take everything that grows on top of the earth and also what grows in it.'

'That's all right with me,' the cow replied.

And do you know what she planted?

Apple trees! Of course! The apples don't grow in the earth or on top of the earth, but up in the air!

So the cow crunched the lovely red apples right under the fox's nose. She was proud to have proved that foxes were not the craftiest of animals.

'Agriculture is quite beyond me,' admitted the sly-boots. 'Foxes' honour, I will never work with a cow again!' he swore, very humiliated.

With that, he went back to the forest to chase rabbits.

The Bored Chick

Little Chick wandered around the farmyard.

He was chased out of the duck pen to the accompaniment of much loud and excited quacking.

Master Cockerel knocked him over without even seeing him, as he preferred to watch the hens.

Mrs Hen, hurrying along followed by her brood, jostled him.

The dog growled because he was tickling his whiskers.

The cat chased him for fun.

In despair, Little Chick went far away from the farm.

He was warming himself in the sunshine near the pond in the village when a lovely glittering creature caught his attention.

'How handsome you are!' he exclaimed. 'What lovely colours your wings are! Who are you?'

'I am beautiful, not handsome,' a piping voice corrected him, 'because I am a lady dragonfly!'

'Miss Dragonfly, will you play with me? Everyone jostles me or chases me away and I'm so bored!'

'What could we play, Little Chick?'

'Catch . . . or leap-frog . . . or racing . . .'

The dragonfly shook her head.

'Come now, Little Chick, I would win all the time!' Forget about those games. But, since you like colours, I will teach you to paint!'

Every day Little Chick went back to the pond where the dragonfly was waiting to give him his painting lesson.

She taught him that by mixing just four colours, red, blue, yellow and black, he could make an infinite variety of shades.

From then on, Little Chick didn't need anyone to play with. He was much happier with his paints and easel.

Barney Finds New Masters

It was raining hard. Barney sat on the pavement and cried because he was wet and muddy and miserable.

Christine came out of school and seeing Barney sitting there called, 'Eric, come and see this dog! He's all wet and he's frozen.'

The two children wanted very much to take Barney home with them, but their father did not want animals in the house.

Eric and Christine ran off home knowing their mother would worry if they were late. It was sad about Barney but his master was sure to come for him soon.

Soon they had reached home and just as Christine opened the gate, something raced between her legs and almost knocked her over.

'It's the dog, Eric! He followed us! What will Daddy say?'

'Come quick, I've got an idea!' replied Eric.

The children took Barney to the bottom of the garden where stood a garden shed.

'We'll hide him in here and later on we can bring him something to eat.'

Christine put Barney in a crate full of old rags. 'Lie down Doggy,' she ordered. 'Wait for us here like a good boy. We'll be back very soon!'

The children hurried back to the house where their mother was waiting with their tea.

It had stopped raining after tea and Eric and Christine rushed into the garden and ran to the shed.

Christine opened the door. The dog was still sitting in his improvised basket and looked at them wagging his tail happily.

'Woof! Woof!' he barked, 'I'm hungry!'

'Be quiet, Doggy, be quiet!' begged Eric. 'Mummy will hear you!'

'Here, eat!' said Christine, giving him bread and butter and some chocolate.

'This is for you too!' said Eric, giving him a piece of meat from the kitchen table. Barney ate the lot in a flash!

'Now, we'll go for a walk,' said Christine. 'But whatever you do, keep quiet!'

Barney crept out of the shed with the children. All at once their mother appeared and called angrily, 'And what is that dog doing here? Ah! Now I know what happened to the meat on the kitchen table!'

'Please don't be cross,' begged Christine, 'he followed us here. He looked so unhappy and he was dying of hunger!'

The doleful look on the dog's face

soon won the mother over.

'Look, there's a name on his collar! Let's see: Bar-ney! His name is Barney and he's two years old, but he is awfully dirty and he's shivering! Bring him into the house!' she said.

'Oh, thank you Mummy! We *are* going to keep him, aren't we?'

'We'll see. If his master reclaims him, we will have to give him back! In the meantime, we're going to give him a good bath! Come along, Barney!'

Barney was not very fond of water and jumped about in the bathtub where he had been put, so much so that they were all completely soaked!

Finally Barney was clean. His eyes were shining and he smelled of soap and lavender because he had had a rub-down with talcum powder as well.

The children's mother installed him on a soft blanket in the linen cupboard and gave him some soup.

'What will Daddy say?' Christine and Eric both wanted to know.

'Don't worry about a thing, children. I will speak to Daddy, and we will teach Barney to bring him his slippers and his newspaper when he comes home from the office! He won't be able to resist him.'

And he didn't, which was good for Barney.

The Duckling and the Circus Folk

Dennis was a tiny duckling, covered in down. He followed his master, Stephen, everywhere. When Stephen went to school, Dennis went too, and waited at the classroom door for him to come out.

The time passed slowly for him. A loud quack! quack! announced his impatience and all the pupils started to laugh.

'Dennis is not to come to school!' ordered the teacher.

The next day, shut in the barn, Dennis was not at all happy. Suddenly he heard strange noises. He slipped through a hole under the door. There were two green caravans on the square. A man wearing trousers with fringes on and a wide brimmed hat was playing the trumpet. A beautiful lady was singing to the music.

'Roll up, roll up! Come to see the circus!'

The caravans had parked on the village green. The doors opened and out came a dog, a cat and some white ducks; who rushed straight to the pond.

Dennis went to join them. In duck language, his companions explained, 'We are performers! You will see us tonight!'

The lady duck said, 'I've got a pink hat with flowers on! The drakes have spotted ties! The dog dances on his back legs. The cat answers questions, and the monkey is an acrobat. There is plenty to see and it's lots of fun.'

'I will come and watch you!' promised Dennis the duckling.

Dennis was a little overawed by such clever ducks. When it was time for the artistes' meal Dennis made his way home. Besides, nobody had asked him to stay and eat. Then he went for a nap in the barn so that he wouldn't be tired that evening.

Stephen arrived home late from school. He had spent a long time on the green watching the circus with

his school friends. He called to Dennis, 'Quickly, come and eat your dinner and have a run. You're going to bed early tonight, and I am going to the circus.

'The circus,' thought Dennis, 'if only you knew! I know much more about it than you do!'

In the evening, so as not to be shut in the coop, Dennis went back into the barn. His head under his wing, he looked as though he was asleep. Quite happy that his pet duckling was safe, Stephen went to the show.

As soon as he had gone Dennis slipped through the hole, and ran to hide in the grass near the performers. There were benches set up round the ring, the lights were shining and the orchestra played. The lady started to sing. It was even lovelier than he imagined. The ducks walked in step, danced to the music, and jumped on the water in a golden pool. They were criss-crossing as they swam, then turned round and round.

Sitting on a star-spangled cushion, the Persian cat answered all the questions. The dog was wearing a jacket and a bow-tie. He danced and twirled, spinning like a real top.

Before the monkey's act, the dog took a collection for the artistes and collected the money in his hat which he cleverly held in his mouth. The acrobatic monkey climbed a tall mast in leaps and bounds. He took a bow, then let go of the mast with his feet and hands and hung on by his tail! In the midst of so many marvels Dennis fell asleep.

Next day, when he woke up, the circus had gone. Dennis went quickly back to the barn where Stephen found him.

But Dennis would not forget his brothers, the performers. The circus would be back next year. He would be older then and would be able to stay awake.

The Naughty Monkey

Chester the chimpanzee woke up very early one morning. He was bored, so he decided to play the fool for a while, as was his wont.

Swinging from a tree he landed with a heavy bump on the scaly back of an enormous sleeping crocodile. 'What's going on here?' asked the crocodile.

'Hello,' said Chester cheerfully.

'Hello!' exclaimed the crocodile. 'I'll give you hello! How dare you wake me up when dawn hasn't even broken yet! It's high time you were cooled down and I'm just the one to do it!'

And with a flick of his powerful tail, he sent Chester flying right into the middle of the river.

'Great!' exclaimed Chester. 'A morning bath is just what I needed. Thanks a lot!' Once in the water, Chester swam fast. He wanted to get back to the bank as quickly as possible for more mischief.

He felt full of beans, and when he caught sight of a boar who was still asleep he was delighted. 'I must wake him up,' he thought.

Finding some long feathers that were scattered on the ground, Chester picked them up and tickled inside the wide ears of the defenceless boar.

The boar woke up with a start and, not realising what was going on, charged off blindly into the nearby forest.

Chester was delighted.

But still the naughty chimp was not satisfied. Chester needed more good pranks to play on the sleeping animals. He started by turning all kinds of somersaults, accompanied by loud and repeated shrieks, then he hung from the branches of the trees and finally fell to the ground and gave himself a big round of applause.

With all the unaccustomed noises so early in the morning, the animals were woken against their will and

felt very bad-tempered. They decided to teach Chester a lesson.

'We'll show him who he's dealing with,' they agreed. And with some of them howling, some screaming, others shouting, whistling, baying or growling, they all rushed to chase the terrified Chester.

'It's time to go,' said the naughty chimpanzee to himself.

So saying, he hurried back to the forest and took refuge among the bunches of ripe bananas, which he used as missiles against his pursuers.

What a commotion that caused. The animals skidded on the fruit and lost their balance, falling on top of each other, geting bumped, bruised and scratched.

Chester convinced himself that he had had a lucky escape, and that was all that mattered to him.

He started to breathe again, to rub his hands with glee, and again to enjoy his life as a foolish monkey. When suddenly a hand seized him.

'That's the end of me,' thought Chester with dread. 'I'm somebody's prisoner now.'

Chester plucked up courage to look at his captor, and with great difficulty had to stop himself from throwing his arms round his neck, he was so relieved. 'Kikou,' he said, in his own language, 'I'm so happy to see you!'

But his best friend Kikou looked very stern. He thought Chester had played too many pranks that morning, and he replied in a deep voice, 'You're coming with me young man, to pick bananas for the family. The other animals deserve some peace and quiet for the rest of the day.'

'All right,' agreed Chester.

He climbed on Kikou's back and walked with him through the forest, looking for the best banana trees.

Bella's Adventure

Mother and Father Beaver were happy. They had three lovely little beavers: Flip and Flop, the two eldest; and Bella, their young sister.

'Stay in the birch wood, darlings, while we go and cut down a poplar to build a dam,' said Mummy Beaver.

Daddy and Mummy Beaver gnawed at the bark of the poplar tree, then at the wood. Watch out! The tree was about to fall. There! It toppled to bridge the river with a loud crash.

'Now, let's bring earth and stones to fill in between the branches.'

The little beavers were playing in the birch wood. They gnawed at thin bark, washed themselves and smoothed their fur.

'Bella, come to the river and learn to swim,' suggested her brothers.

Flop dived first and swam with his webbed paws. He steered himself with his wide tail. 'Well done, Flop!' cried Bella.

'Your turn, Bella, go on, try,' said Flip. 'I'll stay right behind you.'

Bella paddled, splashing and laughing at the same time, then let herself slide in the water.

'Move your paws,' cried Flip. 'More. That's it—you're getting better!'

'Oh, I'm so far out!' exclaimed Bella, a little worried.

'Push with your tail to go back

towards the bank,' said Flop.

'I can swim!' cried Bella as she got out of the water.

She stretched out in the grass to dry off, while her brothers took a turn in the water.

Softly, softly, the fox was creeping up in his fine russet fur. 'Bella, I've got some water-lily roots for you, they are just over there,' he said slyly.

Bella was thrilled and started to follow him. But her brothers had seen the sly fox, and knew the danger, and called out loudly, 'Bella! Come back!'

The two beavers swam to the bank and chased off the furious fox. 'Bella, come now! You know very well that the fox is a liar.'

'Ah, there you are,' said Mummy Beaver. 'Is everything all right?'

Flip and Flop told her what had happened.

'Oh my darling!' cried Mummy, hugging her daughter to her. 'Soon we'll have a house in the water. You'll have nothing to fear from the fox then, and you'll have all the water-lily roots you can eat.'

Bella never trusted the fox from that day on.

The Disobedient Wolf

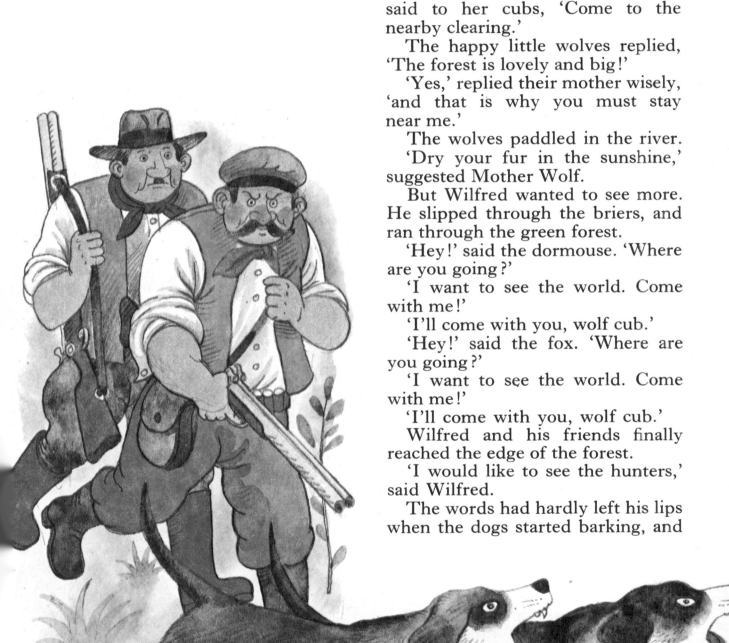

In the spring, Mother Wolverine said to her cubs, 'Come to the nearby clearing.'

The happy little wolves replied, 'The forest is lovely and big!'

'Yes,' replied their mother wisely, 'and that is why you must stay near me.'

The wolves paddled in the river.

'Dry your fur in the sunshine,' suggested Mother Wolf.

But Wilfred wanted to see more. He slipped through the briers, and ran through the green forest.

'Hey!' said the dormouse. 'Where are you going?'

'I want to see the world. Come with me!'

'I'll come with you, wolf cub.'

'Hey!' said the fox. 'Where are you going?'

'I want to see the world. Come with me!'

'I'll come with you, wolf cub.'

Wilfred and his friends finally reached the edge of the forest.

'I would like to see the hunters,' said Wilfred.

The words had hardly left his lips when the dogs started barking, and

159

men came out with their rifles.

'Quick, let's run,' ordered the fox.

The little wolf ran straight ahead through the brambles.

Wilfred was so frightened he did not know which way to go. His paws were torn and hurting him too. He thought he could still hear the ferocious dogs behind him. The dark, safe wood was so far away!

Suddenly a strong hand seized him, then two arms enfolded him. 'Don't be frightened,' said a boy's voice. 'I will save you, little wolf.'

The child ran through the wood, hugging the warm fur of the wolf cub, whose thumping heart slowly quietened down.

They crossed the river together and jumped over the fallen tree trunks. 'We'll go to my hut,' suggested the boy. And there he held the head of the bright-eyed wolf cub on his lap.

Sulking and furious, the hunters went back to the farm. 'It's safe for you to go home now, little wolf.'

Wilfred thanked the child and ran as fast as he could until he found his mother. He threw himself into her arms, and as she stroked him she said, 'My little baby wolf, don't ever disobey me again!'

'I won't,' replied Wilfred.

Zipp and the Bee

Stretched out in the sun, Zipp the lizard was having his nap. He was completely still, and the only movement was his heart beating under his fine skin.

Suddenly a buzzing busy bee passed, whirling like a top. 'What a shame!' wept the bee. 'I have got to make my honey, and I can't find my way back to the hive! My legs are covered in pollen. What will become of me? The Queen will be sure to punish me if I let this precious pollen go bad.'

And she buzzed and moaned so much that she exasperated the young lizard who whipped the wall with his tail in a gesture of anger.

'It's impossible to have a rest in peace. What do you want?' he asked.

'I've lost my hive, I've lost my hive,' the bee moaned again. 'I flew so far to find this precious pollen,

that now I can't find my way home any more.'

'Come, come, calm down, chatterbox!' said Zipp, somewhat more kindly. 'I think that, behind this high wall, I saw a big field scattered with funny little huts, and lots of your kind flying around them.'

'That's it, that's it!' hummed the excited bee. 'But, alas! I am so tired. I will never be able to fly over this high wall and get to the other side.'

'Let's see now,' said Zipp, thoughtfully, 'I know where there's a hole in the wall.'

Gliding nimbly from stone to stone, the lizard soon arrived at a gap, from which there was only a little way to fly. The bee took off and soon found herself on the roof of her hive among her own kind.

She was so grateful that to this day she often goes back to sit next to the lizard and say hello.

James and the Reindeer

James climbed the flowered path that led to the top of the mountain. It was alive with bright bursts of colour on each side as far as the eye could see, and so pretty. He had decided to spend the day at the top of the mountain with his friends the reindeer. The village was just waking. Spring was smiling everywhere, in the gardens, in the trees, and in the streams.

The air was clear, a lark was twittering and was answered by the stream. The boy, not to be outdone, made up a pretty song:

Oh a reindeer I see!
Another! and now three!
Won't you please come here,
My sweet little deer?

James quickened his pace. He was in a hurry to see his friends the reindeer and especially Rudi, who was born only a few weeks ago. He was such a sweet little reindeer that no one could help loving him. James had adopted him as a very special friend.

Up on the mountain the animals were waiting impatiently for the boy to arrive because they loved him very much.

'Will he come today?' Rudi asked his parents. The hours flew by and time passed so quickly when his friend was with them! At least that's what Rudi thought.

'Wait a minute,' said his father, 'I'll see if he's coming.' He looked down the valley, he looked at the mountain slope, he glanced right and

162

left . . . Ah, that little dot . . . Yes, it was James all right, making his way up the flowered path, and singing a song that could just be heard.

'There he is!' he announced happily.

'I can see him now!' cried Rudi, jumping for joy. 'Quick! Let's run to meet him.'

Father and Mother Reindeer followed Rudi, who leaped from rock to rock, like a reindeer possessed, speeding along like lightning.

James caught sight of them and gave an affectionate wave.

How nice it was that all his friends had gathered to greet him! It made him feel less out of breath to see them waiting there!

One, two, three, another few bounds by the deer, a few rapid steps by James, and our friends were finally reunited.

'Hello, I'm so happy to be with you again!' said James.

'Dear little friend, we are so pleased to see you,' chorused the three animals, licking the child's hands.

James climbed on Father Reindeer's back, and it was a pleasure for the animal to carry him, leaping from rock to rock up to the summit.

James's village looked so tiny from way up there. The little houses seemed no bigger than dolls' houses. It looked so funny!

James was hungry and sat down on the grass to eat his lunch. He kindly offered Rudi some fruit. Rudi was always thrilled when his friend brought him new food to try.

'It's delicious,' remarked Rudi. 'Thank you very much.'

Then Rudi grazed on a few sweet, carefully chosen plants, and invited James to go for a ride with them to explore some places he did not know.

'I'd love to,' replied the boy, and he climbed on the back of Father Reindeer, who was pleased to carry him once more.

163

One, two, three, Father Reindeer jumped over the precipices. Rudi followed and Mother Reindeer was not far behind. Now and again, James shut his eyes because the height made him feel giddy.

Suddenly a beautiful sight opened up in front of their eyes. The reindeer, and the boy, all sighed with real pleasure.

'Oh, a waterfall!' cried the boy. 'Isn't it pretty!'

The animals and the child had a drink and cooled themselves down in the clear water.

'It's a magnificent spot,' said Father Reindeer. 'The view from here is wonderful. Look James, that red and white dot is your house.'

'What good eyesight you have!' declared James in wonder. He too strained to see his house. Finally he could distinguish the tiny patch of colour and knew he was looking at it. At this moment his mother would be bringing in the washing, but she was too small to be seen.

The rest of the day went by very quickly with rock climbs and different games, and then the sun decided to go and shine on the other side of the world.

'Toowit toowhoo! my friends,' announced the owl. 'Since I am awake, the night must be coming.'

James thought that he must go home quickly before night fell and asked Father Reindeer to take him.

In a few minutes, the two were at the foot of the mountain, which had turned dark blue.

'See you again soon!' James promised his special friends.

The Girl and the Golden Ring

Dolly, the otter, was very unhappy.

Her aunt, the ferret, had a coat of golden fur. Her cousin, the beaver, was wrapped in an elegant mossy covering, while she was sadly indistinguishable from the grey of the earth!

Dolly was so drab and so small that nobody noticed her. Nobody wanted to play with her. Everyone chased her away, calling her Miss Plain Jane!

It was so terribly unfair! And to escape from her torment Dolly had got into the habit of keeping away from people.

What wouldn't she have given if, for just one day, she could be as beautiful as a film star!

She knew that if only people could forget her plain exterior, they would find she was beautiful inside. But nobody seemed prepared to give her a chance. Nobody was at all interested in the sort of person she really was.

Poor Dolly was never invited to any parties. She would sit glumly at her window and watch everyone else rushing off to enjoy themselves. 'Another evening at home on my own!' she would sigh.

One morning, Dolly had taken refuge behind the stones of the

waterfall. Suddenly a figure appeared, so suddenly that Dolly stared
open-mouthed. Was it an invasion
from Outer Space?

The Beauty with the Golden Hair
was dressed in a gown of field flowers.
Bent over the water, she was drink-
ing. She filled her cupped hands with
fresh water. How pretty she was!

Dolly was so lost in admiration
that she did not feel her feet slipping.
She could not grip the wet stones
and fell into the water. She landed
right in the beautiful lady's hands.

Dolly lay there shaking with fright.
She expected to be told off. And
such a pretty creature would be
bound to think she was hideous. She
would probably drop her in disgust!

'Careless little thing!' said the
young girl, picking her up gently.
Just as gently she put Dolly down
on the bank. Before setting her free,
she kissed her and murmured, 'Go
along, quickly, pretty little otter.'

These words made Dolly blush
with happiness. Until that morning,
no one had ever told her that she was
pretty! Full of joy, she went to hide
in the bushes. How kind and polite
the creature from Outer Space was.
But where had she put her flying
saucer?

The next day, Dolly returned to
the waterfall. She had picked a big
bunch of daffodils. She would give it
to the beautiful stranger as a token of
her thanks.

The stranger was again on the bank of the stream. Today, she was dressed in a gown of moonlight.

Leaning over the water, she was putting butterflies in her golden hair.

Shyly, Dolly held out her bouquet. The beautiful young girl gave a cry of pleasure, and took the flowers from Dolly. She smiled at the anxious face of the little otter. Made bold by the Beauty's smile, Dolly kissed her.

Blushing at her own audacity, Dolly ran off quickly to hide. She badly needed to collect her thoughts.

'Dolly, you're getting very forward all of a sudden,' the otter told herself. Then she exclaimed, 'Whatever has come over me? I'm so shy usually . . .'

The next day Dolly went back to the waterfall. Full of joy at the prospect of seeing the beautiful stranger again, she hummed to herself.

Alas! She found the young girl bent over the water in tears.

Dolly couldn't bear to see her new friend crying, and rushed immediately to see if she could help.

When the girl saw Dolly, she said between sobs, 'My sweet friend, could you please dive in and bring me back my gold ring? It has fallen to the bottom. Without it, I shall never be able to go back to Fairyland.'

167

It took Dolly a long time to locate the ring which was buried in the sand.

To get it out Dolly had to dig for a long time. She stayed under the water much too long. Dolly resurfaced and gave the young girl her ring. Exhausted, she fainted in the fairy's arms.

The beautiful fairy looked down at the creature who had so generously endangered herself for the fairy's sake.

The young fairy blew on Dolly, and Dolly came back to life. She opened her eyes with a sigh, flushing with pleasure. But, otter's honour, she would never set foot in the deep water again!

The fairy gave Dolly a kiss, then disappeared as mysteriously as she had arrived. Just then, a shower of beautiful flowers fell on Dolly. What magical colours!

Dolly watched the flowers with amazement. She tried to catch them, but as she touched them, they melted. Then she looked at her own reflection in the stream.

Under the rain of flowers, Dolly's fur had turned gold. Then, all at once, she started to grow. She was transformed by the magic of a fairy. And she became beautiful.

Dolly went home and her Aunt Ferret and Cousin Beaver were both green with envy.

For the sake of a fairy and a gold ring, Dolly hard learnt to swim.

The Copper Cauldron

One morning, Catherine's grand-mother decided to clear all the use-less things out of the attic. She sorted out a pile that she put into a wicker chest and sold to a trader who was passing.

When he had unpacked every-thing, the trader noticed that there was a hole in the bottom of a little copper cauldron. He decided to sell it all the same and it wasn't long before he did just that. Catherine recognised the cauldron and bought it for a moderate price. She took it home and polished it until it shone brightly.

'Oh!' cried Roderick, Catherine's tame squirrel. 'It's just like a mirror!'

'Yes,' replied Catherine, 'but un-fortunately there's a hole in the bottom.'

'I'm sure my friends the beavers will mend it,' said Roderick.

The girl and the squirrel hurried off into the forest where the beavers, having seen what was needed, set to work.

Artistically, they scraped the bot-tom of the cauldron with their flailing tails. Catherine made up a fire to melt a little piece of copper. Then they spread the liquid copper over the bottom and waited for it to dry.

Catherine went home and put the cauldron on the sideboard where it was admired by everyone.

The Drowning Moon

It was a warm blue night, beautiful, and sparkling with stars. The moonlight was so lovely that one longed to be outside.

Sally could not resist the temptation. As soon as she had finished her dinner she went walking into the garden full of flowers.

'How fragrant the air is, how pretty everything looks,' thought the girl as she walked towards the round goldfish pond.

Sally sat at the edge of the pond and dipped her hands in the water. She felt so good and so happy that she thought nothing could disturb her.

But something did disturb her. She heard a voice mumbling beside her, 'I'll never do it, I'm sure, I'll never be able to do it.'

'Georgina, what are you doing?' Sally asked her friend in astonishment.

A strange friend to be sure, a pretty frog who was twisting and turning this way and that to fish something out of the water.

'Have you lost a water-lily leaf?' asked Sally, laughing.

Georgina stared at the girl with tears in her eyes before retorting, 'If only that were all! Can't you see that it's drowning!'

Sally became worried and bent

over the water, obviously ready to help, but all she could see was the reflection of a round shining moon.

'Well,' said the indignant frog. 'What are you waiting for? The moon is drowning!'

Sally looked at her friend and burst out laughing before she said, 'You're so silly! The moon is in the sky.'

'No! It's not,' replied Georgina. It's drowning!'

She jumped up and down with rage, missed her footing, and found herself in the water.

'Croak! Croak!' she cried. She looked at the clear water again, and then stared at the sky. How can it be that the moon is drowning in the water and be up there at the same time? It was impossible. It was a trick. She had never seen anything like it!

But Sally explained it to her. She fetched an earthenware pot and moved it little by little until its shadow made the reflection of the round moon disappear.

'Oh, croak!' choked Georgina.

Sally took the pot away and the reflection reappeared as clearly as before. 'You see,' said Sally. 'I was right.' Georgina was so pleased the moon wasn't drowning that she felt in the mood for a game. The two friends played hide-and-seek in the garden. Georgina couldn't find Sally. 'Croak, croak, I give up.'

'All right,' said Sally to please her, 'we'll play jumping if you like.'

But Georgina lost at that too, and she was not in a good mood after that. 'I've had enough,' she declared.

So Sally decided to go for a walk. Nothing seemed to please Georgina that evening!

The Kitten Who Hated Carrots

'Dinner's ready,' called Mother Cat.

Marmaduke pulled up the chairs to the table.

Thomas put out the napkins.

Benjy took a piece of bread.

Patch, the hungriest one, was already holding out his plate.

'Just give me some potatoes, I don't like carrots!' said Patch.

'You will eat your carrots the same as your brothers!'

'Carrots are nice,' said Benjy.

The little cats tucked in to their meal.

'Patch is getting no dessert until he empties his plate. Here's the rice pudding!'

Patch watched his brothers enviously.

'Close your eyes,' advised Marmaduke.

'Then swallow the carrots,' said Benjy.

'It's impossible!' Patch pulled a face.

'You three go and play,' said Mother Cat, 'there's a present from Uncle Cornelius for you.'

'Oh!' cried Marmaduke, 'a cowboy outfit!'

'Oh!' cried Thomas, 'an Indian outfit!'

'Oh!' cried Benjy, 'a redskin brave's outfit!'

Patch was getting anxious about his present. He grabbed a big spoon and ate all the carrots.

'You haven't left any for me!' said Mummy.

'I thought I had to eat them all!'

'Very well,' replied his mother. 'Here's your pudding.'

But Patch wasn't hungry any more. He rushed to open his parcel.

And that is how Patch became the Big Chief of the Indians.

Herbert the Hippopotamus

Herbert the hippopotamus was snorting in the river. He was dozing off in the sun after his bathe. The water ran down his gleaming skin. Herbert was proud of his easy-going gait, and headed slowly for the bank, when a playful fish slipped in between his legs.

'Stop it, Cyril!' he grumbled, having recognised the joker.

But Cyril wanted to have fun with Herbert. He hindered his progress so much that the hippopotamus stumbled on a stone and crashed with all his heavy bulk into the clear water which splashed up all around him.

Cyril was not spared; he turned suddenly into a flying fish!

But it was a bad fall and Herbert panicked. 'My left leg is wounded. I can't walk any more!'

Cyril was in despair. It was his fault that his friend was in such pain. He called to his brother fishes to help. 'Hey, fellows! Go and fetch Carla, Herbert's mate. She's the only one who will know how to look after him.'

Straightaway, all the fishes went off to look for her. They searched in vain. Carla seemed to have disappeared!

Cyril could stand no more. He

left two of his companions to look after the invalid, and went himself to look for Carla. He found her eventually in a thicket, eyes half closed, lazily sniffing the fragrant flowers.

When she heard of the accident that had befallen her mate, Carla slid into the water at once and hurried to his side. She pushed him up on to the bank and cried in her gentle tender voice, 'Oh, my poor Herbert! Don't worry. I will look after you!'

The fishes had prepared a mixture of underwater plants which had great healing powers. Carla applied the correct dosage and started dressing the painful leg.

They did not have to wait long for the treatment to take effect. Herbert stopped groaning at the first application, and soon a contented snoring shook his huge chest.

'I feel better!' he sighed with a yawn. And, as his reassured friends watched, he stretched ponderously and calmly resumed his interrupted nap.

175

The Hare, the Tortoise and the Kite

One fine summer's day, the hare laid a wager that he could reach the other side of the field before Mrs Tortoise. But he dawdled on the way and lost.

He was very annoyed and determined to get his revenge. He declared to his adversary, 'My good woman, I bet I get to the top of that hill ahead of you.'

The clever tortoise accepted the challenge, on condition that the race was held on a day when the wind freshened the air. The hare agreed. As it happened, the very next day there was a strong wind. So, at the signal, the hare started to run up the side of the hill.

Meanwhile, Mrs Tortoise went to see her friend John Barley, the farmer, and asked him to lend her the kite that he had just made. The farmer agreed, and hooked the tortoise on to the tail of the kite and released it.

A few minutes later, the tortoise floated down on to the top of the hill. And when an hour later, the gasping hare arrived at his goal, Mrs Tortoise gaily called to him, 'What's the matter with you, Master Hare? You look very weary, yet it was a most agreeable run, don't you think? I've been waiting for you for the last hour!'

Three Little Pigs

One fine summer morning, the three little pigs on the farm looked scrubbed. They were brushed and glowing all pink.

'Oh!' they said. 'Look, everyone, how handsome we are!'

And the three happy little pigs danced and admired themselves in the clear water of the pond.

The grey donkey who was watching told them, 'Silly pigs, you're going to the market.'

'Well then, we'll go for a walk,' replied the three little pigs. 'And we'll go on the swings! And we'll eat sausages grilled in the open air!'

'No, you simpletons,' the grey donkey went on. 'At the market the farmer will sell you. And then . . .'

The three piglets did not want to hear any more. They ran behind a haystack and whispered in each other's ears. It was not easy with ears as big as theirs, but this was a serious matter.

They didn't like the idea of being sold at the market, when they were so happy on the farm with all their friends!

'We must think of something,' said one of them.

All the animals gathered together: the cows, the horses, the foal, the grey donkey and his son, the sheep and the lambs, the turkeys and the guinea-fowl, the hens, the cockerels, the ducks and the dogs.

'We are leaving at dawn tomorrow morning,' one piglet assured them.

'The horse's harness is all polished,' added the second piglet.

The three piglets, all pink and clean, washed and brushed, had heavy hearts. They did not get a wink of sleep all night, tossing on the fresh straw.

The dog barked and the cocks crowed. Would they ever hear them again?

Poor little well-scrubbed piglets! 'That's one! And two! And three!' said the farmer putting the three piglets into the horse cart. The three piglets were swung up by one leg and their tails, squealing loudly.

All the animals watched them, tears in their eyes and fear in their hearts.

At the gate, the grey donkey was waiting and called to them, 'See you soon, my friends. See you soon!'

And he flapped his big ears mysteriously.

The horse trotted at a good pace along the sunny road, which smelt of ripe hay and summer flowers. But the three piglets, piled together, shaken and buffeted about, were so sad that they did not smell the fragrant air.

They did not see the luminous blue sky or the bright pretty road. In fact they did not see anything.

Where are they going to end up?

'Come along, Duke,' croaked the farmer, cracking his whip. 'What's

the matter with you?'

The horse walked slowly and thought, 'Who cares about the whip!'

'Duke, gee up. Go, Duke! Gee up!'

But in the wood Duke slowed down, then stopped altogether. He hung his head as if he couldn't take another step if he tried.

Surprised, the farmer jumped down, stroked the horse and examined him. 'Is one of your hooves hurting? Let me see.'

The horse did not move.

'Well, I don't know. I've never seen anything like it! I'll have to get help.'

The farmer tied the horse to a tree and went off alone down the road. Straightaway, the horse cried, 'Hey, don't go to sleep up there, you three numbskulls. I'm not hurting anywhere really! Quick, take the road to freedom!'

No need to be told twice. One! Two! Three! The piglets jumped on to the road and vanished into the wood. There they met the wild boars who would be their friends and give them acorns and roots to eat.

Ever since that day, on market days, when the farmer and his wife have gone, the three piglets come to visit their good friends at the farm. How happy they are then.

The farmyard rejoices.

Everyone hugs and kisses and dances and sings.

Don't let the night come too quickly!

The donkey tells them all the news.

But, watch out, the farmer will be back soon. Shhh! Don't breathe a word to him!

Bunny Rabbit

'I've got a rabbit!' cried Helen.

But Bunny-Rabbit lifted his nose and hop! He jumped right off that hutch.

'Bunny-Rabbit is missing!' Helen cried.

Bunny-Rabbit had slipped behind the garage.

'Give me the watering hose,' suggested Robert.

Bunny-Rabbit, terrified, did not understand what was going on.

When Robert grabbed him he was a wet rabbit, soaked through.

Helen rubbed him with a towel.

At last Bunny-Rabbit shook himself. He rubbed his paws over his face and his long ears. He gave himself a good wash and stretched out in the sun to dry.

It was safe in the hutch.

The Lost Fox

Little Desert Fox was very unhappy. He desperately tried to poke his long pointed snout as far as possible through the bars of his tiny cage. His enormous frightened black eyes darted from right to left. His big velvety ears pricked up at the slightest sound. His whole being was on the alert.

Alas! He was a prisoner. He was captured by some men whose job it was to hunt animals, and then shipped in a stifling hold of a boat. How long was it since he left his native Sahara?

Night fell on the docks. The cages that were piled up there would soon leave for the cold towns of the north. Desert Fox could not bear to live locked in a zoo. He struggled like mad and crash! His fragile prison swayed and smashed on to the ground. Desert Fox was quite giddy but he was free.

He took his opportunity immedi-ately. He picked himself up, shook himself, tested his legs to see if they were all right, then took off before anyone found he was gone.

The fox ran as fast as he could on his slim paws. Roads stretched out before him, the town passed by, but he did not even look, he was so intent on escape.

Finally, out of breath, he stopped. The singing of the birds and crickets, the smell of flowers and grass, told him that he had reached the country. He lay down exhausted in a hollow...

A warm ray of sunshine tapped

181

on his eyelid. Little Desert Fox opened one curious eye, then the other. His memory came back to him and, happy to have escaped from a life of misery, he started to dance among the marjoram and thyme.

A few wild rabbits came to stare at the strange animal.

Infected by the fox's high spirits, one by one they joined in with him and danced nimbly to the music of the grasshoppers and the crickets. Voles, hedgehogs and shrews all watched them with amusement. Desert Fox, lost to the world, turned a few more pirouettes before he noticed that everyone had vanished. Two children, Miriam and Vincent, were coming along singing.

'Why, hello, rabbits!' called the children. 'Have you found a new friend?'

The rabbit who seemed to be in charge spoke up and told them about the fox's experiences. Miriam and Vincent were troubled. While they gave him tit-bits, they pondered the situation. Desert Fox would not survive the winter so they must persuade him to accept the hospitality of the nearby zoo, where the animals lived almost free. There he would find open spaces and a nice warm enclosure. The fox was easily talked into it as he knew deep in his heart that he would never see his burning desert again. Anyway his new friends had promised to visit him.

One fine morning, Desert Fox sat with Miriam and Vincent in their grandfather's cart, among the flowers for the market. His heart was light and he was making plans. A lady Desert Fox was waiting for him at the zoo.

The Outcast Frog

One beautiful spring morning, on an enormous water-lily leaf, a frog gave birth to two babies.

There would have been nothing unusual about that, but one of the little girl frogs had almost white skin. What is more, she was very pretty and had lovely golden eyes.

Mother Frog was very proud of her babies and looked at them with admiration and affection. But the dowager lady frog, who was sedate and wise, came to get a closer look at the strange phenomenon. She adjusted her glasses several times, tossed her head and declared in a knowing tone: 'She is an outcast among us; we can't possibly accept her.'

The mother frog intervened on behalf of her white daughter. 'Let me keep her, just until she doesn't need me to look after her any more.'

'I will consider it,' said the old frog.

Then she gathered the other frogs together, who all approved of her decision.

The days went by, and the white frog became a little beauty. But no

one except her mother and her sister would talk to her; everyone else ignored her.

One fine day the little frog decided to go away. She could not bear being an outcast any longer.

She went to the beavers and asked if they would build her a raft. The obliging beavers set to work immediately. They wished her good luck as she boarded it and floated off with the current.

The frog arrived near a bank that looked inviting and she decided to spend the night there. But at dawn, she found that the raft had been carried away by the current; so the only sensible solution was to stay there.

The local inhabitants were charming: field-mice, cuckoos, orioles, they all admired her and thought the

frogs had been very hardhearted. 'They are not only mad, they must be blind as well,' they said when they heard how the white frog had been treated.

Then they built the newcomer a beautiful house and decorated it with an abundance of moss and masses of flowers. And so a pleasant life began for the young frog.

One day the frog decided that it was high time that she found a husband so she asked the orioles to find one for her, as she knew no reptiles like her in that part of the world.

The orioles returned with a light grey, golden-eyed frog who fell in love with her immediately.

The wedding took place amid great rejoicing and the white frog lived happily ever after, and had little frogs of her own.

A Weasel in Peril

Miss Weasel had put on her gold slippers and her pretty red dress, and had set off into the very heart of the forest.

'Oh, my poor aching feet!' she cried on the way back. 'I don't think I can walk another step.'

Joe, the majestic white swan heard the complaint. 'Hey there, Miss Weasel! What's the matter?'

The weasel went up to the big calm lake on tiptoes. 'Master Joe, my paws are bleeding; I've walked so far!'

'That's what happens to irresponsible youngsters,' Joe replied pompously. 'Why don't you soak your painful paws in the water!'

She followed his advice and Miss Weasel soon felt better. The two of them chatted, and Master Joe complimented the weasel on her pretty dress. His kindness even prompted

him to carry her over to the other bank on his back.

'Joe must be mad!' cried the other swans. 'Look at him chauffering that ugly creature about!'

Miss Weasel put one trembling leg on to the bank. Her face was bright red with shame. She pondered the whole evening on the way to silence the cruel tongues of the swans. By morning, she thought she had the solution. She returned to the lake with a crown of flowers on her arms.

'Master Joe, I award you the Order of Merit for services rendered to a weasel in peril.' And she placed the crown on his head!

'Permit me, madam, to take you on a tour of the lake!'

And Miss Weasel, delighted, glided elegantly past the other, very disconcerted swans.

The Performing Seals

A small circus was installed in the main square of a large town for the whole summer. The most remarkable act in the show consisted of three performing seals. They danced, jumped through hoops, turned amazing somersaults, juggled with big balls, balanced on the trapeze and played the trumpet. It was such fun to watch them doing their act.

A sweet boy called Stephen thought that they were so good that he did not miss a single show. Each time he went to the circus he slipped into the wings where the animals were kept, and talked to the three seals, giving them a friendly stroke. As a treat he always brought them a pail of fresh little fish, which they loved.

In short, Stephen and the seals were the best of friends, and were very pleased to see each other every evening. A month went by in such a manner and they were all happy.

Then suddenly, Stephen was not to be seen at the circus for a whole fortnight. The seals were very worried about it.

Could the boy have forgotten his friends? Had he been forbidden to go out as a punishment? Had he moved away from town?

One evening, the circus master gave his troop a day off. What joy to be free for a few hours! The seals decided to go in search of their friend Stephen, and to explore the town until they found him.

They wandered for a long time through the town. They finally ar-

rived in front of a house where a pale and sad boy was standing at the window. It was Stephen! They were so happy to see him again after such a long separation.

'I have been very ill and I am still not quite better, so I'm not allowed to go out. I just don't know when I'll be able to come and see you at the circus again,' explained Stephen sadly.

'Don't worry about it, Stephen. We've got a lovely surprise for you,' said the seals, and rushed away.

They went to fetch all their instruments from the circus and returned to Stephen's house as soon as they could.

That evening they put on the finest show ever seen for the sick boy.

Stephen would never forget that wonderful act of friendship.

188

Sweet Bosso

The jungle was still asleep. The sun hadn't yet put out the first tip of its beam when something terrible happened to Gillian the giraffe.

It seemed impossible, even incredible, but unfortunately it was true. Some men had captured her and were taking her to a famous zoo in Europe.

It wasn't hard to realise why they had done such a thing. Gillian was very beautiful, and would be one of the main attractions for the zoo's visitors!

As she stood shut in the lorry taking her to her new life as a captive, Gillian wailed very loudly, 'Who can help me get out of this? Help!'

The animals, who were half-asleep and bewildered, watched her getting further and further away. But at once the news spread like wildfire. 'Gillian has been captured!'

In his round hut, Bosso was asleep. The day was not old enough for him to get out of bed . . . not until the smell of the coffee that his mother was brewing roused him from his slumber.

Bosso stretched on his mat and sniffed, 'Hey, that smells good!'

'Bosso!' cried his mother, 'I've just seen Gillian in a lorry!'

'What!' exclaimed Bosso, stunned. He drank his coffee so fast that he burnt his tongue, then he swallowed a piece of warm millet cake. He had a

quick wash in the river then ran to see his friend Mambo, the garage owner, who owned a fast car.

'Gillian has been captured!' Bosso panted.

'He's right,' confirmed a spotted hyena. 'They captured her at first light. I saw it myself.'

Bosso and Mambo acted quickly. They started the engine and got into the car with the hyena sitting between them.

'We must catch them up,' cackled the hyena.

That is exactly what Bosso and Mambo intended to do.

Suddenly Bosso shouted for joy. 'There's the lorry!'

'Go get 'em!' cried the monkeys, who were following the chase with interest, by leaping from tree to tree. A few even managed to find a seat on the boot of the car.

Mambo pressed harder down on the accelerator and they soon caught up with the lorry.

'Stop, thieves!' cried Bosso very angrily.

Bosso jumped from the moving car, determined not to let the men get away. Mambo was right behind him.

The men took fright and tried to run away. But the nimble monkeys acted too quickly, and tied them up with the ropes the thieves used to catch animals. Then, just to round things off, the thieves found themselves well parcelled up in the cages meant for Gillian and their other victims.

Mambo and Bosso burst out laughing and couldn't help poking fun at the prisoners: 'What strange beasts you are!'

Gillian laughed heartily showing all her teeth, and took Bosso home on her back.

'I will visit you tomorrow,' Bosso joked. 'Just to make sure you haven't been captured again!'

Billy Bear's Fine Catch

'Aaah!' said the fox, settling himself comfortably under a tree in the clearing among the golden ferns. 'This is just right in the shade for a little snooze.'

'Shush!' said Mother Fox to her children. 'Go and play somewhere else. Your father is having his nap.' The happy fox cubs leaped about under the trees and ran races round the bushes.

Meanwhile Billy the bear cub, his rucksack over his arm, set off fishing and muttered, 'Father thinks I'm lazy. Well, we'll see! All my brothers are playing leap-frog but I'm going to bring back some fish for dinner tomorrow.'

Merrily Billy followed the path

that led to the bank of the river.

Dragonflies skimmed overhead and butterflies hovered over the flowers. But Billy only had eyes for the river bed. With a quick flick of the paw he had caught a lovely big trout.

Billy cheerfully carried on fishing and did not notice the sun going down on the horizon.

But Mother Fox had. 'Hey!' she said, shaking her husband Ferdy. 'You've slept long enough. It's time to go hunting.'

Ferdy opened one eye, then the other. Rubbing his snout lazily he stretched. 'Ah! How nice it is to stretch like this in the sun!' said Ferdy with a yawn.

Evening was on its way but Ferdy fell asleep once more.

Not until the sun had hidden behind the big trees did Ferdy Fox shake himself. But it wasn't the dark night that made him do so. 'Well, well,' he said. 'I smell fish. Perhaps Father Bear has been fish-

ing?' The smell of fish was coming from Billy, who had a full and heavy rucksack. He had put it down for a minute to play hide-and-seek with the fox cubs.

'It's not fair,' said a fox cub, 'you always win, Billy, because you can climb up and hide in the trees! Still, you will come back and play tomorrow, won't you? Promise?'

'It's a promise,' said Billy.

When Billy got home, it was very late.

'Your father is already in bed,' Mother Bear said to him. 'He is furious because you were not home. Now eat your soup quickly and go to bed without a sound.'

Disappointed at not being able to show Father Bear his catch, Billy hung the full rucksack in the pantry and locked the door.

Jumping out of bed with glee next morning, Billy cried, 'Dad, come and see my surprise!'

'Hmm!' replied the bear. 'What

have you been up to this time?'

Billy rushed to the pantry and took the rucksack off its hook. 'That's odd! It feels so light! Why, it's empty! Who has taken my fish?'

In a fury Billy went off into the forest. There he met his friend, the wild boar.

'You look very cross, Billy,' remarked the boar. 'Whatever is the matter?'

'Someone has stolen all my fish.'

'Well! Well, I never! How awful! Wait a minute, though, I've just remembered! It seems that Ferdy the fox is ill. He's got a fish-bone stuck in his throat . . .'

The bear cub followed the wild boar and listened as he accused the fox of stealing Billy's fish.

Ferdy had to confess his guilt.

The wild boar and the bear cub gave him a well-deserved telling off.

'And now, Billy, you can go fishing again. You'll see; your father will be proud of you!'

Sooty and the Doll

Stephanie had been given two beautiful presents for her birthday that day. One was a doll that she called Jessica, and the other was a little grey-black cat. He was adorable with his big blue eyes, and Stephanie called him Sooty.

What a cheeky thing Sooty was! While Stephanie played with her doll, he would run all over the place, scratching the armchairs and clawing the curtains, and all of it at top speed. Stephanie's mother did not take too kindly to his sort of playfulness and she asked Stephanie to teach Sooty some manners.

Stephanie undertook the task willingly. While she cuddled her doll, she coaxingly explained to her Sooty that he must not do such mischievous things.

'Miaow, miaow,' replied Sooty, who couldn't care less about his sweet mistress's advice. Stephanie had to fight the urge to let him do as he pleased. He was so funny, so cheeky and so happy, that it was really a shame to make him keep quiet.

The following Wednesday, when Stephanie's friends came to tea,

Sooty felt sad. He was not allowed to play with Jessica, the doll, and no one paid him any attention.

It was then that Sooty made up his mind to be like a doll himself. That evening he would not play. In the morning he refused his milk, and shut his eyes.

Mother called the vet, who reassured her. 'There's nothing wrong with Sooty but he seems a little sad.'

Stephanie put down her doll and cuddled Sooty. She even coaxed him to follow her into the garden.

And what jumping and miaowing, what energy Sooty had then!

He was happy now, no longer jealous of the doll.

Theo and the Alarm Clock

Theo was the name of the nice boa constrictor at London Zoo. Good natured and totally without malice, Theo spent most of his day digesting his food.

Theo had a voracious appetite. It was his biggest failing. And consequently he often suffered from indigestion.

Once his friend the vet had been very cross with him, and put him on an all-day fast! But still Theo was very fond of the doctor. Whenever he could get out of his cage, Theo went to the vet's office to visit him. He curled up comfortably in the armchair, nestled snugly into the cushions, and dozed off.

One day, Theo did not feel at all well. It wasn't that he had eaten too much. This time he had caught the 'flu. He was not the only one. The surgery was brimming over with patients. Oh dear, there wasn't much room for Theo! Theo was shivering with fever as he looked at the doctor.

The doctor wondered what to do

with Theo. Then he put him into a basket and went off to ask his wife.

She suggested that she should look after Theo, and nurse him so that he would get well quickly.

Theo was put into a linen basket. He was nice and warm, next to the radiator. It was heaven! Theo wanted to get better, of course, but not too quickly.

He swallowed his spoonfuls of syrup like a good boy. The only drawback was that he wasn't allowed to eat. Although his stomach was upset by the 'flu, it suffered more from hunger.

That afternoon, the doctor and his wife went out shopping and Theo soon became bored. And the more bored he got, the hungrier he became.

Theo left his basket and went off to explore his new world. Finally he arrived in the kitchen. At last, he was going to be able to eat something!

But . . . no luck. The washing up was done and the left-overs of the meal thrown away. As for the fridge, Theo just couldn't open it!

Very unhappily, Theo went back to his basket. He tossed and turned on his bed, trying to get to sleep.

Tick, tock! Tick, tock, ticked the alarm clock, making fun of him! Theo got more and more cross. Because of that noisy alarm clock, he couldn't get to sleep and forget his hunger. That mean alarm was making a terrible racket!

Theo stretched out his neck and

swallowed it. And how he suffered for that, children!

For that wasn't the end. Tick, tock, tick, tock, the alarm clock went in Theo's stomach. Oh, how bad Theo felt! His whole body was shaken by the ticking and tocking. And his stomach rebelled at this very noisy lump of metal.

Imagine the astonishment of the doctor and his wife when they returned home! The alarm clock that Theo had swallowed started to ring. It made Theo's head vibrate. As his jaws chattered, his eyes almost popped out of their sockets. And to cap it all, they were laughing at him! Poor Theo was on the point of fainting away.

The doctor, with his wife's help, hurriedly opened Theo's mouth. The indigestible object popped out of his throat. What a relief!

Theo soon forgot his nasty moment as he tasted some milk and honey, and a piece of cake, while all the time the vet's wife affectionately stroked him. Full of happiness, Theo finally went to sleep, but not before he had stuck his tongue out at the alarm clock.

Flick the Squirrel

'The time has come for us to collect our stores for the winter,' said Mother Squirrel in the nest up the big oak tree, one autumn day.

'We'll go,' cried the squirrel children. 'Flick, come with us! Why don't you help us, instead of playing the clown in the branches?'

'But I'm an acrobat!' replied Flick, who was the youngest.

The hedgehogs, the weasels and the rabbits egged him on: 'Bravo, Flick!' In the evening, the brothers came in tired, and complained, 'Flick never brings anything in!'

'I'm collecting stores of songs and stories,' replied the little squirrel, who didn't believe winter would ever come.

But come it did. Snug inside his nest, Flick crunched sweet hazelnuts. 'The snow is sparkling with thousands of diamonds, how pretty!' 'Yes, yes, but will we have enough to eat?' his brothers fretted. 'You haven't done a thing to help!'

'Don't worry, I will tell you stories that I collected from the old owl!'

The glow-worms shone in a garland and moonbeams filtered through the trees. The squirrels forgot their empty stomachs.

'Now I'll go and pick stars,' promised Flick. 'I am giving a party for you.'

The crickets brought their guitars, and the grasshoppers fetched their accordions.

Flick recited poetry, and the rabbits danced.

'What a wonderful party, Flick!'

Flick was happy to have brought happiness to the tree. He was a magician! With him, it would be easy to wait for spring and his brothers forgave him for not collecting any nuts.

Honey's Long Ears

At Clearbrook Farm, three adorable golden puppies had just been born. Mother Spaniel was so proud of them that she gave them the prettiest names she could think of—Beauty, Topaz and Honey.

The months went by and the puppies grew much bigger, but their mother was worried about Honey. Her ears had grown faster than the rest of her, so that they looked enormous, and trailed along the ground. They knocked over everything in their wake, including the farmer's flower pots and the cat's saucer of milk.

Mother Spaniel never knew what Honey was going to knock over next. Every time she heard the clatter of something falling in the farmyard she would call out, 'Honey! Is that you?' And more often than not, a shame-faced Honey would come trotting up and say, 'Yes mother.

I'm sorry. I'll try not to do it again.'

At night, nobody could sleep because the long, long, ears tickled noses and made them sneeze.

Mother Spaniel could not console the poor dog about her deformity.

One morning, Honey had had enough. A cheeky little mouse had just bitten her left ear with his pointed teeth. She could not go on like this!

The young dog raced at full speed back to the house and complained to her mother.

'Don't cry any more, Honey. When you are fully grown your ears won't seem nearly so big. They'll be the same as all the other dogs'!'

'Why do my ears have to be so long? Other animals have long beaks, long legs or long teeth without causing any trouble. I'm going to ask their advice!' she said to herself.

So Honey went into the flowery meadows. It was a beautiful day and the foals were prancing about happily in the sunshine.

Their long legs were kicking high. Honey greeted them warmly and asked, 'Why have you got such long legs?'

'To be able to run faster, you silly thing!' they said, galloping off.

Disappointed, the puppy went to the river where she met two beavers, who were gnawing at some wood with their long, pointed teeth.

'Hello! Why have you got such long teeth?' she asked.

'We use them like saws,' replied the beavers. 'It's a pity we haven't got ears as big as yours or we could use them as oars!' the rascals mocked.

More and more disheartened, Honey lay down by the river to sulk. Just then a green frog jumped on to one of her ears and, thinking it was a rug, settled down comfortably.

Then, two kittens who happened to be there, laughed so hard at the comical scene that they fell in the water.

'Help! Help!' they miaowed.

Honey dived into the river without hesitation. She told the kittens to climb on to her ears and she would swim to the bank with them.

When all the farm animals heard the story, they congratulated the brave and clever puppy, and organised a big party for her.

Now, Honey has grown into a beautiful dog with perfectly normal ears and no one has ever made fun of her again.

Good Friends

Early one morning, Laurence set off to pick mushrooms with a cane in his hand and a basket over his arm.

As he passed the big field where the cows were grazing, he greeted them kindly. 'Good morning, ladies, I hope you are well!'

The cows answered him with moos that the child translated as 'yes, thank you'.

Laurence headed towards a little wood where he knew he would find juicy mushrooms. He was already looking forward to eating them. Mummy knew how to cook them so well!

As Laurence started picking, he caught sight of something striped under a bush. It was not a mushroom of course. It was a badger, a wounded and very distressed badger.

'I got my paws caught in a trap,' said the badger in a voice weak with pain. 'If you looked after me, I could get better, you know.'

Laurence didn't waste a minute in taking his new companion, whose name was Barry, home with him. There he nursed him for many days.

He made a bed for him to lie on, with blankets to keep him warm. He fed him with bread and milk at every meal. Each night he changed the bandages on the badger's paws.

Soon Barry Badger got quite well again and, one morning, he told Laurence that he wanted to go back to the wood. 'Nevertheless,' he reassured his rather sad friend, 'we can still see each other every day in front of my home.'

The child and the badger returned to the forest only to be met with a terrible problem. Barry Badger's home had been filled with earth.

'What will become of me now?' cried the troubled badger.

Laurence comforted him, and promised to help him rebuild his house. But that was no easy task as Laurence and Barry Badger soon found out.

As soon as they had cleared the earth away, some more fell in. They decided to find a new location for Barry.

The two friends found a free space near Crafty Fox's lair and decided it would do nicely, but Crafty barked, 'I don't want any neighbours!'

They met with the same thing further on. 'Hey!' protested Red Hare. 'My children need plenty of space. I have first option on this mound.'

Laurence was annoyed and said, 'You're not real friends. You don't know how to please someone else!'

The fox and the hare couldn't care less about the badger's lack of a home, and Laurence tried to console his little friend. 'We'll find you a place, you'll see. You mustn't give up hope yet.'

And it was not long before they did find a place. Laurence and the badger both spotted a pleasant site, thick with ferns.

There were no animals living nearby to complain that Barry was building on their territory. It seemed ideal. 'Just what we need, let's get to work!' they cheerfully cried out together.

Earth flew all around them as they dug. The little ferns could not get over being tossed hither and thither.

'I'll plant you again,' promised Laurence. 'The main thing at the moment is to build a home for my friend Barry Badger.'

The ferns tossed their greenery in scorn and indignation but Barry and Laurence ignored their tantrums. Time was passing much too quickly for their liking.

The two friends worked very hard without a break, singing a happy song that Barry made up:

'Cheerfully dig the soil and loam,
We are building Barry a home,
We are building a spacious hall,
Where all our friends will come to
    call,
And every night we'll hold a ball.
Cheerfully, cheerfully dig down
    far.
And forget how tired we both are.
Tomorrow morning, we may reach
    the end,
Ready for you to move in, my
    friend!'

Laurence turned red with his efforts, and Barry got very dirty, but both of them were in a good mood when night fell. They had already built a passageway and a room for Barry Badger to store food.

Then Laurence flopped to the ground with a big yawn and Barry plumped down next to him, absolutely worn out.

'We'll have to carry on tomorrow morning,' said Laurence as he stretched out on the grass to rest.

Barry Badger thought that was the best idea too, and he wiped his paws on some nearby leaves.

The next morning, with the first warm rays of the sun, Laurence and the badger set to work again with renewed vigour.

Soon they had built a room beautifully lined with moss. Then several other rooms with emergency exits followed on. The whole thing looked splendid.

'It's as grand as a castle,' said Laurence proudly, clapping his hands in sheer delight.

And Barry Badger thought so too.

There was still more work to be done though. Stores for the winter had to be collected, and Barry Badger set to work once more, with Laurence helping as best he could.

Day by day, the storeroom got fuller and fuller, and when winter came Barry Badger said good-bye to Laurence. 'We will see each other next spring. Thanks for everything!'

'I'll be thinking of you all the time,' the child promised his friend.

When the snow sprinkled its first flakes on the forest it brought with it winter sports. Laurence took part in them while he waited for spring to return.

When it did, the child ran to Barry Badger's home. He was sure to come running when the child called him!

'Barry, little friend, I'm here! It's me, Laurence!' he shouted.

But, oh dear! Although Barry Badger was not far from his home, he was deaf to the call, because he was with a lady badger.

'I don't believe it,' thought Laurence sadly. 'Barry Badger has forgotten me!' And dragging his feet, he set off slowly towards home, not even bothering to pick the pretty primroses on his way.

Some time later, however, when Laurence was playing hide-and-seek with his friend the cuckoo, Barry Badger came quietly up to him.

'I've got something to show you, Laurence. Come with me.'

And what a surprise it was. Laurence was quite speechless! The badger had got married and had four lovely children.

'Congratulations,' said the boy affectionately. 'They're all adorable.'

And every day the badger family had great fun playing games with Laurence.